Bimbo Fixati
Kimmy Vere

ALL RIGHTS RESERVED: No part of this book may be reproduced, stored in a retrieval system, or transmitted, in any form or by any means, without the prior permission in writing of the publisher, nor be otherwise circulated in any form of binding or cover other than that in which it is published and without a similar condition including this condition being imposed on the subsequent purchaser. Your non-refundable purchase allows you to one legal copy of this work for your own personal use. You do not have resell or distribution rights without the prior written permission of both the publisher and copyright owner of this book. This book cannot be copied in any format, sold, or otherwise transferred from your computer to another through upload, or for a fee. **Warning:** The unauthorized reproduction or distribution of this work is illegal. Don't do it. Criminal copyright infringement is investigated by the FBI and is punishable by up to 5 years in federal prison and a fine of $250,000.
Publisher's Note: This is a work of fiction. All characters, places, businesses, and incidents are from the author's imagination. Any resemblance to actual places, people, or events is purely coincidental. Any trademarks mentioned herein are not authorized by the trademark owners and do not in any way mean the work is sponsored by or associated with the trademark owners. Any trademarks used are specifically in a descriptive capacity. All characters should be assumed to be over the age of 18. They all give some form of consent (including tacit). The cover model is also over the age of 18. **Cover created Shutterstock imagery.**

First Edition
©2016

Contents

Chapter 1..4
Chapter 2...15
Chapter 3...29
Chapter 4...46
Chapter 6...79
Chapter 7...102
Chapter 8...126
Chapter 9...155
Chapter 10...176

Chapter 1

Her fingers curled as she contemplated destruction.

She wanted to punch him. Hard. She wanted to punch him hard and kick him into the wall. She'd smash his laptop and his stupid PowerPoint presentation.

Unfortunately, Sabrina needed to be polite for now. The guy at the front of the conference room kept going on about revenue growth rates, cash burn, and search engine optimization. Sabrina knew his type, a pretty set of shoulders in an expensive suit. She really, really wanted to punch him.

He'd probably cry.

But he wasn't one of her employees, so she couldn't do much. Like it or not, she needed these investment bankers. They had the licenses and relationships necessary to take her company public.

Exhaling through her nostrils, she tried to release the stress pounding in her temples. When that didn't work, she leaned back in her chair, allowing the banker drone to continue his inane points. He was talking about cash flows now, and Sabrina seriously doubted that anyone else in the conference room really paid attention to this guy.

And yet, this was a ritual. They had to go through these formalities.

How would I feel right now if I was just a bimbo?

Sabrina furtively glanced at the other people in the room. Currently, there was only one other woman, Janet, another investment banker of some kind. Some of her attention was drawn toward Stephen and Michael, two of her employees. Stephen handled internal security while Michael focused on public perception.

Yeah, Sabrina wasn't especially worried about either one right now, and yet she kept spinning back to that same question.

How would I feel right now if I was just a bimbo?

Sabrina could feel her lips tighten and her skin redden. She was slowly becoming aroused, especially when she stopped to think about bimbos. She saw them throughout her life, in middle school, high school, college, and in virtually every office she had ever visited.

They seemed ubiquitous, those airheaded girls who could just twirl their fingers through their hair, smile, and act all ditzy. Those girls didn't really contribute anything, but they all seemed so happy. The guys liked them too.

Not Sabrina.

Outwardly, she hated bimbos. She hated the blonde nitwits who gave all women in professional contexts a bad name.

And yet, Sabrina could imagine herself as some dumb girl. She could be a secretary or an executive assistant in a short skirt with a tight top that pushed up her breasts. She would struggle to follow along, only to get bored and reach over to touch one of the men. Maybe her hand would drift down to his crotch, and she would rub him.

Yes, that would be so much more interesting. She could stroke him, and if he got really excited, maybe he would excuse himself. Then Sabrina could do the same, and she would scurry after him. He would take her back to his office, and he would shove her up against the wall. He would kiss her, he'd strip her, and then he'd take her hard.

"How does that sound, Ms. Riley?"

Ms. Riley. Someone was talking to her. Sabrina blinked, and she looked back around. The investment banker in the front of the room had apparently finished his presentation.

"Ah, very informative," she said, her tone both neutral and utterly detached.

The banker glanced around the rest of the room, perhaps searching for some kind of cue from her colleagues. They just shrugged back at him. Everyone in that room who knew Sabrina understood one very basic fact about her. She didn't worry about being nice. She focused entirely on success, and if she didn't view any member of her team as essential, then she'd ignore him.

Sabrina remained in her seat as the investment bankers left of the room.

Michael leaned over. "You know, we need them."

"We need their connections and their expertise. The man himself was clearly an idiot."

"This is going to be a fairly small IPO, so maybe we should try to tread lightly? It's not like all of the banks are falling over themselves for our business."

Sabrina wrinkled her lips together, pouting ever so slightly. She stared back at Michael, and he shrank back an inch or two. Even so, he was accustomed to dealing with the owner of this company.

And he had skills, Michael wasn't going to get fired.

"Perhaps," Sabrina allowed. She pulled out her phone and checked for the information on the next meeting. "Michael, it seems that you are going to be presenting next. Apparently, we have a PR problem?"

"Yes."

"Should we talk about it now?"

"I'd really rather wait until we can get everyone in here," he said, glancing back toward the doorway. He probably wanted to take out his phone as well, to check the time if nothing else.

Most of the employees at this company became very nervous when left alone with Sabrina. Unlike so many other bosses, she wasn't especially cruel or vindictive. No, she was just utterly focused and completely professional.

Lots of other managers fell into one of two categories. They could be vicious little despots, or they could be hypocritical politicians. That second group always tried to pretend that coworkers could be the best of friends and that a company's success had to be the most important thing for everyone.

Not Sabrina. While she demanded competence, she didn't ask for any kind of unique passion or dedication. She understood that everyone came into that office to succeed at a specific objective.

It was the kind of cold detachment of that made Michael hit his pen against the tabletop.

Several other employees showed up, and Michael cleared his throat. He went over to the whiteboard. "We have a problem, ladies and gentlemen. Currently, we are negotiating to enter the final phases of our initial public offering, but that has meant lots of the bloggers are upset."

"Why should we care?" Sabrina asked.

"They do provide the bulk of the content for the website," Michael replied.

The website. He didn't speak of the name aloud. Pretty much everyone at the office understood that Sabrina didn't enjoy talking about their brand. The website had a simple name, Giggle Girl. This lifestyle and fashion website catered to women with an interest in the superficial.

Sabrina never said it aloud, yet it was obvious. And her business model was very simple. She exploited all of those bloggers who didn't mind writing elaborate articles for just a few dollars. As far as she was concerned, this is capitalism at its finest.

"Content is at issue," Sabrina replied. "If they don't want to write for us, they can write for someone else. They're always going to be more bloggers out there."

"True," Michael agreed. "However, we still need to be worried about the question of public perception. We employ a lot of bloggers. If they all get upset with us at the same time, they will start spreading rumors. They won't stay quiet, and then we might have a much larger PR issue."

"Our readers don't care about fair pay."

"Ms. Riley," Michael began carefully, "I know that you are in charge, and this is your publication, but you hired me so that I can help you with this sort of blind spot. The fact is that we don't know what will happen if we have a mass revolt on our hands. You're right. We can probably get more writers without much difficulty. But if we get a chorus of former employees crowing about how terrible we are, our readers might defect. There are lots of other content portals they could visit instead of us."

Sabrina leaned back in her seat. She touched her fingertips together. In that moment, she really did look like some super villain, perhaps a billionaire heiress with a plan to melt the Arctic ice caps.

"Michael, please draft an email to all of our bloggers. Remind them that we appreciate all of their contributions. Also remind them that Giggle Girl is built on a chorus of voices. No single individual is a more important than anyone else, and if anyone wishes to go it alone, we wish them nothing but the best."

He hesitated. Finally, his shoulders slumped, and he sighed, "I can do that."

"You will do that," she corrected.

"I will," he promised. "But maybe it would be a good idea to consider the revenue sharing plan that some of their leaders have suggested?"

"They have leaders?"

"Yes."

"Don't fire them, but I do want to them phased out. Move all of their articles to the lowest traffic areas of the site for one week. After that, tell them that we will no longer have need of their services since they aren't able to generate the kind of numbers that we expect."

He opened his mouth, and it looked like he wanted to say something, but then he stopped. "Yes, Ms. Riley."

The other employees filed out, but Sabrina just reached over to her tablet computer. She opened it, and she minimized the various spreadsheets. At this point, she had absolutely no interest in dealing with the accounting. Just the idea of numbers was enough to make her eyes ache.

After a quick reconsideration of her schedule, she opened up a book on her tablet. The story played along the screen in digital letters. She allowed herself to relax into the soft narrative.

It felt good.

This particular story was simple. It was erotic and intense, but it felt like a soothing balm for her psyche.

Sabrina didn't really understand why. She spent some time online, poking around various discussion groups, but she never saw a satisfactory answer for what might cause her particular desires. Why would she be so interested in this concept?

She was sitting there, after all, reading about a brilliant scientist who was drugged against her will and turned into a big breasted, blonde haired, idiot bimbo. As her eyes played along the screen, her lips tensed, or skin warmed, and she could feel that comforting pulse of desire right between her legs.

She was getting wet.

Really, Sabrina shouldn't have done this at work. If she wanted to get herself excited, she should have waited until she was home or at least alone in the privacy of her office.

But those meetings...They drained something for her. They were so excruciatingly boring, so simpering and stupid.

And yet, they also brought her a little bit closer to the success she was supposed to crave.

"What are you reading?" came a voice, snapping her out of her fantasy reverie.

Sabrina brought her computer back up to her chest, and she tried not to look like a high school girl caught with some illicit material. Even so, the color drained away from her cheeks, and she stuttered. She stammered something idiotic. "Schedules," she finally forced out. "I was just looking up some schedules for content releases."

"I see," he said.

That's when Sabrina realized this man was standing within line of sight of her screen. There was a good chance he saw exactly what she had been reading.

Sabrina opened her mouth, wondering if she should say something about it, and then she changed her mind. No. She was the woman in charge here, so if she wanted to read some illicit material, then she would do it. It was none of his business.

"What's your name again?"

"Cale Larsen," he said. "I'm acting as a consulting attorney for the IPO."

"Cale, you would be very wise to focus on your job performance and nothing else. I don't tolerate incompetence within my company, even from consultants. You understand?" She was grateful those words didn't shake or break as she spoke.

"Absolutely," he said.

She got up, she smoothed out her skirt, and then she left the room. At the same time, she felt the blush curl along her cheeks once again. She didn't know if she was thinking about the bimbo scientist or the guy who caught her.

As she made her way back through the office, Sabrina marveled at everything she had built here. Normally, she didn't focus on sentimentality, but to this point maybe she needed a little reminder.
The office space was modern, with lots of open work desks. People could roll around and chat with one another. Her programmers routinely did this. The office had once been a warehouse or a factory. Exposed brick and wooden beams adorned the different walls, and huge chunks of industrial equipment could still be seen overhead.
Of course, there was still a geeky feel. This place was largely inhabited by computer programmers and other assorted nerds. As she walked by different desks, she noticed Super Mario figurines, a Serenity model, and at least one bust of Lara Croft.
There was a larger section of the office that could only be reached via ladder. At some point, she was probably going to get in trouble with the ADA, but Sabrina didn't care. That would be one more lawsuits could deal with down the line. For now, no one noticed.
Sabrina climbed up to that second level, and she looked out at the rest of her employees. This was it, her miniature empire.
Back in business school, she spent a lot of time talking with some of the other proto-entrepreneurs. For many of them, this was definitely the dream. They wanted to get a start up going, a company that could attract investors, and change the world.
"Two out of three isn't terrible," she whispered to no one in particular. She leaned out against the railing, watching as her employees worked and typed and coded and programmed.
She didn't change the world. She had a freaking website called Giggle Girl. And even if it made money, it definitely didn't make the world a better place.
Did she want to handle the world problems?
No, not really.

Sabrina just wasn't one of the more optimistic grad students who had believed in social entrepreneurship. She figured that business could be about making money or helping the world. She didn't understand how both things should happen at the same time. Anyone who tried to aim for both goals was just kidding themselves.

She heard the telltale clanks of footsteps against the ladder.

A young man with dark hair popped his head up. He climbed the rest of the way, and he approached without the same reservation as her other employees. "What is it, Kyle?"

"Marcus and Danielle are here to talk to you."

"And I bet Michael wants in on this meeting as well?"

"You guessed it," Kyle answered. He leaned forward on the railing as well. Sabrina glanced back over at him, enjoying the sight of his shoulders. He had on a dark gray sweater made from some stretchy material that highlighted his best features.

Pretty soon, she would have to venture back down onto the main floor, she'd have to go to the conference room, and she'd have to endure another interminable meeting. Apparently, lots of executives like her suffered from tremendous stress just before the IPO. And yet, bringing this company public would make her rich, really rich.

But did she care?

Back in business school, money was supposed to be everything. All of her fellow students loved talking about what they would buy or what they would do. There were so many dirty jokes and incredible fantasies.

Her phone buzzed, and she pulled it out, checking to see that an email had arrived. She didn't recognize the name, however, so she was about to stow it back in her pocket, thinking this was another bit of trivial business. But then, she saw something important, the subject line.

I know what you want. The email came with an attachment.

"Should I reschedule your meeting?"

"No. You can tell them that I'll be down in a little bit. Oh, and Kyle?"

"Yes?" Somehow, this guy always managed to sound so delightfully energetic and pliant. He'd be happy to do anything and everything she desired.

"Don't leave early without talking to me. I might have need of your extracurricular services," she told him.

"Yes ma'am," he answered.

Sabrina had another meeting to survive.

Apparently, there was another twist to the PR problem. Most of their bloggers were women, which made sense considering that the website was dedicated to fashion, health, celebrity, and other rather trite topics. Sabrina didn't respect the content they provided, but she didn't need to. As long as their writers could put up the numbers she required, then everything worked out just fine.

But because she refused to share any of the revenue, it made the company seem somehow hostile to female workers.

Sabrina rubbed the bridge of her nose, and she came up with a different solution. Rather than set a precedent by increasing the revenue sharing model, they would make several donations to women's and feminist organizations. It would provide for a nice distraction.

Speaking of a nice distraction, Sabrina called an end to the meeting, and she went right back to her office. Before she stepped through the door, she sent a message back to Kyle.

Her assistant and boy toy showed up just a few minutes later.

"Have you had a rough day?" Kyle asked.

"I have," she said. "Shut the blinds."

He tapped a button, and the automated covers slid back down in the position granting them a degree of privacy. Sure, the other employees probably knew why she had hired Kyle in the first place, but if executives and CEOs across the country could enjoy themselves, then Sabrina could as well.

Yes, she was definitely a model feminist.

She kicked off her shoes, and she rested her feet on another chair. "I'd like a massage," she told him. She wiggled her toes in his direction.

A slight smirk touched his lips. If he felt demeaned or embarrassed by his position the company, he never let on. Then again, as her assistant, he also had access to some rather lucrative stock options that would vest the moment of the IPO went through.

He sat down on that same chair, and he lifted up her feet, resting on his thigh. Kyle began to massage her, working his fingertips along her ankles, over at the arches of her feet, and against her toes.

At first, he was very gentle. It was almost enough to make her smirk. Sabrina closed her eyes, and she rested her head back against the edge of her chair. She closed her eyes, and she surrendered it to those sensations. He did a good job. Maybe Kyle didn't know a whole lot about spreadsheets or programming, but his hands moved magically over her toes and heels.

"Enough," she finally said. She stood up, she hitched up her skirt, and she pulled down her panties. She set them neatly on her desk. "Lock the door."

"Yes, ma'am," he replied.

The first time he did this, acting all obsequious and subservient, it triggered something within her. This time, it just felt good. But there was no particular thrill, no rush of excitement.

Keeping his head bowed down slightly, he came up to her, and he got down on his knees. He leaned in, and she ran her fingers through his hair. It felt good, really good. She took a firm grip for just a moment, and then she relaxed it. She leaned back again, making sure to keep her legs spread.

Kyle started to lick her. He moved his head down and up gently. She closed her eyes, embracing those sensations. Warm and wet, firm and easy. It excited her, the tip of his tongue playing along the contours of her most sensitive spot.

After a few more seconds, Sabrina glanced down at her assistant. She ran her fingers through his hair, petting him. That had to be demeaning, but Kyle didn't seem to mind. As far as he was concerned, he just wanted to do a good job.

His head moved from the left to right, then up and down. He swirled the tip of his tongue over her slit. He teased her button, and he lapped at her like an eager little dog. But that's how she saw him, more as a pet, more as a puppy than anything else.

Sabrina kept waiting for that surge of excitement. It didn't come.

But it felt good, so she relaxed, taking this as something of a corporate perk.

Once or twice, Sabrina had even ordered him to use his mouth on her while she conducted business. Getting eaten out certainly made her conference calls much more interesting and enjoyable.

But this wasn't really doing it for her.

She didn't tell him to stop. It still felt good, but there was something else she needed, something more.

Chapter 2

After Kyle left, Sabrina went back to her laptop, and she checked the myriad of messages waiting for her. None of them seemed particularly pressing. One of her engineers wanted to know if they could upgrade the server. Someone else was concerned with potential breach, maybe some kind of phishing attack.

She was just about to close out her email tab when she saw it again, that one subject line.

I know what you want.

"Not likely," Sabrina whispered, double-clicking on the message. Chances seemed good that this was just going to be a waste of her time, but she was going to head home, and maybe this would be some kind of corporate proposal.

At that moment, Sabrina wondered if maybe she should just sell her company to one of their competitors. She could make them pay. A lot. That would be pretty satisfying, especially considering that she had to endure quite a few insults for her site.

Yes, she knew that Giggle Girl was silly, but that didn't mean she wasn't serious about her goals. Little by little, she attracted more and more readers, more and more focus. Lots of advertisers wanted to be on her site. Hell, she had some of the best sponsored content on the entire web.

So she could still defend her work, even if she wasn't inherently proud of it. Since it belonged to her, no one else was allowed to insult it.

Those thoughts all flashed through her head as she opened the email.

Her computer started to act strange. The attachment was automatically opened and downloaded. She tried to cancel. It all happened too fast. Before she knew it, a tab opened on the screen requesting that she open this file.

Something like this wasn't supposed to be possible. Unlike so many other websites, Sabrina took security extraordinarily seriously. She had one of the best IT departments of the city. More to the point, she even had boots on the ground in the form of Alexander and his various contacts.

Something like this wasn't supposed to be possible, but she didn't panic. Instead, she looked back at the body of the message.

I know what you want. You want to lose control. You want to change your life, but you're scared. That's okay. Open the file and have a taste. You won't regret it.

Sabrina crinkled her brows as she read the message several more times. It was that second sentence that kept drawing her attention back.

Like so many other women, Sabrina occasionally fantasized about being taken. She might daydream that she would be kidnapped and turned into some harem girl, perhaps an obedient sex slave. But it would always feel so good. She would learn to love her newfound position.

She tried not to think about it, but sometimes she wondered what it would be like if the IPO failed and her company went bankrupt.

Every time an idea hit her, she waited for some surge of fear, a burst of dread that would make her shiver or squirm in her seat. But it never arrived. As hard as she tried, she couldn't get upset over the notion of failure.

Sabrina couldn't articulate exactly what that might mean about her entire enterprise. Or maybe she just didn't want to connect those logical dots.

She went back to the tab. She just had to click on it to open it, and this file would activate in its entirety.

It had already been downloaded. Sabrina disconnected her laptop from the Internet. This way, if there is a virus or something else malicious, she would only lose one computer. And she had plenty of those.

Exhaling, she pushed on the button, and the screen changed instantly.

The icons along the bottom disappeared. Everything turned bright blue, then dark green, then a hazy shade of pink. Those colors flashed quickly, dancing with hundreds of pixels.

Sabrina didn't look away. In fact, she *couldn't* look away.

All of her thoughts dissipated, turning fuzzy, hazy, and utterly indistinct.

Normally, Sabrina saw the world as a series of cause and effect relationships. If she wanted a particular output, she simply had to find the right input. This might mean writing up a resume or drafting a proposal or intimidating an employee. But it was always logical and explicit.

Not this time.

Sabrina kept staring, and the computer program began to work, pulling all of her focus and attention away from the real world as she drifted off into the soft embrace of fantasy.

She sees his face, but she can't remember his name. He has dark hair, a strong jaw, and dark eyes. There is something dangerous about this man, something powerful. He's taller than her, and she already knows that if he walks right up to her, she will shrink back.

He intimidates her.

Sabrina can't remember the last time anyone intimidated her. Even those investment bankers just blustered. They could talk about how they were the masters of the universe. As far as Sabrina was concerned, that just meant they were masters of self-deception.

She is standing in front of the mirror, applying the last of her makeup. She touches the lipstick to her mouth, and he comes up behind her. She is almost naked. Yes, her bra and her panties protect some modicum of her modesty, but they both know he could command her to strip.

And she would obey.

As hard as she tries, Sabrina can't recall his name. Instead, there is just one title, one word that comes to mind when she looks back at him. "Master," she says, dipping her body down.

"Sabrina," he says. "I wanted to talk to my favorite bimbo slave."

"What can I do for you, Master? How may I serve you?" On some level, she remembers that she supposed to be an articulate, intelligent woman. She's supposed to run a successful company. But here, with this man, in this fantasy, she knows her place.

"You can do as you're told. Right now, I want you to hold your hands behind your back while I touch you. I want to examine you. I want to inspect my property."

She gulps, but she obeys, crossing her wrists just above the small of her back. She stands straight, knowing full well that her body is on display for this man. At moments like this, she really does feel like property. She swallows, and then she feels it, that collar around her neck. It's a symbol as well as a reminder.

Her Master circles her, trailing his fingertips along the contours of her body. He touches her stomach and her sternum. He brushes the back of his knuckles just below her breasts. She shivers, and she feels it.

That first spark a desire.

Whether she wants to admit it or not, Sabrina is getting aroused.

Her Master must know this, but he doesn't remark on it. Instead, he comes up behind her again, and he squeezes her ass. His hands glide over her flanks, and then he cups her breasts. Even through the scant protection of her bra, he can clearly feel her nipples. They have stiffened.

"Do you need to think for yourself?"

"No, Master."

"Do you need to make any decisions?"

"No, Master."

"What are you?"

"I'm yours, Master. I'm your bimbo and your slave. My job to please you, Master."

Every word feels automatic and absolutely truthful.

"Good. Take off your panties and touch yourself for me."

Her lips part.

Despite all of her training, this kind of command still makes her shiver with embarrassment. Sabrina has never been the kind of girl who can masturbate on command. But this man owns her, and she needs to please him! She has to be a good girl, or she'll be punished! Rather than disappoint her owner, Sabrina pulls her hands away from the small of her back, she hooks her thumbs into the elastic of her panties, and she tugs that garment down in one smooth motion. She bends forward, and her Master slides his fingers along the curves of her ass. She shivers, but when she stands, she parts her legs, and he wraps his arms around her frame.

Her Master holds her without limiting her range of movement. "Lick your fingers first."

She blushes brightly.

He knows exactly how embarrassing this is for her. She still has that mental block somewhere inside of her head that tells her she shouldn't be a bad girl. She shouldn't masturbate, especially while someone watches! But his authority over his bimbo slave is absolute, so she licks her fingertips, and then she slides her hand back down toward her pubis.

She rubs her fingertips along her opening, stroking gently. She caresses her outer lips once, twice.

He watches, and she whimpers, knowing full well that his eyes are on her. Occasionally, he looks down the length of her body. At other points, he simply studies the mirror before him. He enjoys seeing that little pout on her mouth. Sabrina thinks she's better than this. But she isn't. That's why she has the collar around her neck.

Under his watchful gaze, she glides her fingers over her opening. She moves her fingertips lightly at first, but then he reaches down, and he takes her fingers. He pushes them in deeper. "Enjoy yourself for me. Feel free to moan."

She shivers at those words. Sabrina still wasn't used to being property. She doesn't know how to answer, especially as the pads of her fingers play along her button. The arousal simmers and kindles deep inside of her body, but she is getting closer and closer.

"Master, may I, may I have an orgasm?"

"Not yet," he says. He is still holding onto the back of her hand, guiding her digits down and up, down and up, down and up. He sets the pace for her, and this only adds to her desire.

That desire quickly turns to desperation.

"Stop."

Her hand freezes. She's a good girl. She'll do anything her Master wants.

"Good girl," he says. "Lick your fingers clean for me."

She inhales and exhales, gasping through his command, yet she obeys nonetheless. She lifts her fingertips up, and she starts sucking. He watches her, and then he unhooks her bra. He pulls off that final garment, leaving his bimbo slave standing there in nothing but her collar.

"Are you a smart girl?"

Sabrina continues to suck on her fingers, and she shakes her head. She gives him the answer he expects, the only answer that could possibly be correct.

No, she isn't an intelligent young woman. She's a dumb girl, and she knows her place. She knows that she needs her Master to tell her what to do, to command her every decision.

"Good."

He takes her hands, and he crosses them at the small of her back. That's when he touches his fingertips to her lips. He's very careful not to smear her makeup. Sabrina knows what he expects, so she opens her mouth, and she takes his digits. She swirls her tongue around her is fingers. She sucks gently.

Then he brings his hands back down to her breasts, and he starts to massage her. He touches her nipples, and that first second of contact is like a shock of electricity. She tries to pull back, but he is still holding her there in front of the mirror. There is nowhere for this slave girl to go.

"I enjoy fondling you," *he says, his voice teasing.*

"Yes, yes, Master!"

He continues to play with her, gliding his fingertips along her nipples. Then he pinches them ever so slightly, and it is almost enough to get her off. Almost.

"Master, I don't think I can take this!"

"Of course, you can. You're my possession, so you'll take whatever I give you," *he answers, whispering those sharp words into her ear.*

More than anything, she wants to contradict him, yet she can't. She knows her place. She's been so thoroughly trained that she remains right there, shivering as he fondles and teases and taunts her with one touch after another. Each stimulus feels like it's about to drive her insane, but she remains there. She keeps her legs taut. She can't allow herself to fall.

"Such a good girl. Such an obedient bimbo," he tells her. "Are you wet right now? Are you hot and wet and horny?"

"Yes!"

"Good. Go over to the bed and lay down. Spread your arms and legs. Remember, you aren't allowed to touch yourself."

Sabrina is so grateful! She spins around, and she darts across the room like a little deer running across a meadow. She falls down onto her back, she raises her arms, and she spreads her legs.

Naked, this position leaves her incredibly vulnerable, but she doesn't mind.

She lifts her head a few seconds later. "Master?"

"What is it?"

"Are you, are you going to come and play with me?"

"Not yet," he says.

Sabrina bites down under her bottom lip. She's trying hard, really hard to be patient, but her pussy is throbbing for attention. Those desires keep swirling, and every second feels like a special kind of torture because she needs relief. She's horny! Really, really horny!

But she doesn't whine, and she doesn't complain. Instead, she stays right there, down on her back, waiting for her Master.

Slowly, he turns back, and he walks over to the foot of the bed. He gazes down at his property. "You're not going to move without permission, are you?"

She swallows. She might be able to guess where this is going, and she doesn't like it.

"No, Master. I would never disobey you."

He smirks.

She feels so small, so helpless, especially now. Technically, there is nothing but her own obedience holding her down, yet that's plenty. She inhales and exhales, her heart pounding away in its cage. Sabrina doesn't know what she's supposed to do or say. She doesn't know exactly how to get what she wants.

There's a good reason for that. She can't. There's nothing this bimbo can do. She's just a dumb girl, so she has to wait for her Master to make the decision. "Stay there," he commands, and then he walks out of the room. He closes the door behind her, and

Sabrina actually starts to pull and twist, almost like she struggling against invisible shackles. But really, there's nothing holding her down.

Whimpering, she remains in place like a good girl.

Every second feels like a special sort of torment, a compacted punishment. Those moments ate at her psyche, but there's still nothing she can do about it.

She locks her teeth together, inhaling and exhaling. She tries to calm herself down, but she is so desperate. Granted, it would be easy to lift up her hand, to slide her fingers between her legs and get that orgasm, but she won't do it.

She needs to be a good girl. She needs to be an obedient bimbo.

Concentrating entirely on her Master, Sabrina contemplates what he wants from her.

Eventually, the door opens again, and there is her owner. He walks up to the foot of the bed once again, and he tilts his head to the side. "Who is my obedient girl?"

"Me!" Sabrina chirps. "I am!" The yearning inside of her body actually shifts her tone to a higher pitch. She sounds younger, sweeter, so much more innocent and definitely eager. There's nothing she won't do for this man.

Her Master stands there for a few more seconds, cocking his head to the side. He is utterly confident in his ability to control this girl. They both know it, just as they know she will yield to everything he demands.

"Please, would you like to touch me? Would you like to use me?"

He doesn't answer her directly. "Close your eyes, Sabrina." He uses her name, and a shiver of desire reverberates through her body. She can feel that tracing echo of sensation in her toes, and her fingers, and along her palms.

Obediently, she choses her eyes. Again, she nibbles down into her bottom lip, waiting.

Anticipation is a different kind of torture, and she doesn't know what to do.

Actually, that's not true. She knows what she must to do. She must obey. She must wait there like a good girl.

Her Master opens the closet door. She can hear the rollers. A few seconds later, she feels his weight on the bed. He dangles something above her chest, letting it slide just above her skin. The soft air sends goose bumps along her body.

"Don't fight," he commands.

"Never." She's close to breathless even though he has barely touched her. Then she feels the first cuff loop around her right wrist. He handcuffs her to the bed. Another metal shackle loops around her left wrist.

He's only halfway done.

Her Master uses another set of restraints on her ankles. Soon, she is spread out, and he touches her, brushing the back of his hand from her sternum down her belly, through her pubic hair, all the way down to her slit.

"I love it when you are all wet and eager," he tells her.

"Thank you, Master."

"What you want me to do to you?"

"Use me," she says.

"Not yet," he replies. He straddles her, and he leans down, kissing her forehead. His mouth is so soft against her skin. He barely touches her, yet those sparkling tingles still run through her skin. "Struggle."

Sabrina doesn't need to be told twice. She starts pulling against her restraints. "Just think about what I could do to you right now. I could touch you down here." He fingers her gently, barely slipping his finger into her slit. "Or I could leave you here. What do you think of that, Sabrina? Should I leave you on the bed for a couple of hours?"

She swallows, this audible gulp. And that sound seems to fill the entire room.

Sabrina isn't so arrogant or cocky to think that he wouldn't do it. If he wants to discipline her and punish her and tease her and humiliate her and reinforce authority over her, then he will do it. He'll leave her right there, chained down to the bed and utterly powerless.

By his command, she starts to struggle. He's teasing her, and she knows it, but if she doesn't do a good job, if she doesn't please him, then maybe he really will punish her. Perhaps he will leave her right there...

No, that notion is enough to make her shake with dread. And yet, her pussy is still throbbing. She could feel that tension coil through her body. She yanks as hard as she can against the handcuffs, and the edges dig down into her wrists. She doesn't care. She embraces that sharp little sensation.

In the meantime, he leans down, and he starts to kiss her. He presses his mouth into hers, and she shivers at his touch.

It doesn't last long enough. He moves his lips down to her neck. He nips at her, dragging the edges of his teeth over her skin.

"You'll have to do better than that," he chides.

She bucks and thrashes, fighting so hard. She gasps through every breath, but it still isn't good enough. "Fight."

She groans and growls, especially when he brings his lips down to her nipples. He starts with the right one, licking and swirling the tip of his tongue over that button. He plays with her, and she yields completely.

"You belong to me," he says, breaking contact for just a moment.

Then his lips come down again, he is taunting her left nipple. He licks and sucks, tightening his mouth around her bud. A gasp escapes her throat. She arches her back, and she is so close to an orgasm, yet she resists because she has no choice.

Sabrina needs to be a good girl. She needs to be obedient. She holds onto that truth, and he keeps going. His hand drifts down to her slit, and he fingers her, sliding one digit into her crevice. He toys with her clitoris, watching as she struggles.

Like a good slave, Sabrina still has her eyes closed, but that doesn't matter. She has no trouble at all imagining her Master above her, watching and studying her.

Every second offers him even more insight into her mind and her body. He watches the way she shudders. He studies the sounds she makes. In time, he's going to use all of this information against her. He's going to make sure that she learns how to succumb.

"You belong to me, Sabrina. You don't need to think for yourself. All you need to worry about is putting on cute little outfits so I can show you off to my friends and to my colleagues. You know, they're all very jealous. They have these wives and girlfriends who try to think for themselves. It's all very tiring for them. But I don't have to worry about that, do I?"

Sabrina knows that she must answer. "No, Master."

"And why is that not a problem for me?"

"Because I don't have any opinions, Master. You tell me what to think! You tell me what to do!"

"And...?"

Her heart pounds, one and two; Sabrina really doesn't know what the correct answer is supposed to be. "I don't know," she confesses.

"Good girl," he tells her, and he keeps his hand right there between her legs. He touches her, a little bit faster, a little bit harder. The pleasure builds, and he keeps his eyes locked on hers. "Remember, you aren't allowed to come. Don't have an orgasm."

She holds onto that command; she clings to those words.

Her fingers tighten into fists, and she tries so hard. She must do this. She must demonstrate to her Master that she can be utterly obedient, even when he is cruel and sadistic with the application of pleasure.

When he pulls his hand away from her pussy, Sabrina doesn't know if she should be grateful or disappointed. Her body shivers again, shaking, and she can feel the red lines along her wrists.

But she did a good job. She didn't climax, not without permission.

"I think you deserve the chance to orgasm now," he tells her. He sounds so seductive, so incredibly powerful as those words hit the air.

Sabrina presses her lips together as he starts to strip. He pulls off his shirt, his shoes, and his socks. He removes his pants and his boxers. Soon he's naked, and she sees his cock right there.

"I'm not going to take my time with you. I'm not going to leave you wanting any longer," he says. He positions himself above her. He slides forward, thrusting his cock into her waiting orifice. He fills her up, moving his shaft 1 inch at a time until he's buried to the hilt.

For her part, Sabrina gasps. Her breathing has turned to frantic, but she still manages to speak. "Thank you. Thank you, Master!"

Gratitude pours from her lips as he pushes and pulls, sliding his body against hers. The friction of flesh on flesh is enough to drive her wild. She pulls against her shackles, both those around her wrists as well as her ankles. Her body becomes tense, and those sensations vibrate through every inch of her body.

She loves this. She loves having her Master on top of her. She loves knowing her place. She has been subjugated, and she's grateful. She wants to please this man more than anything. She has no choice.

He kisses her even as he pumps her. Then he breaks away, and he looks down into her beautiful brown eyes. He reaches forward, and he strokes her soft brown hair. This girl is so beautiful, so gorgeous, and she knows that she's absolutely appreciated. She's a cherished possession. She loves being his little sex slave, his obedient bimbo. She loves every moment of it, even at times like this, when he's using her and there's nothing she can do about it. She might pout, and there might be adorable little wrinkles at the corners of her mouth, but that will only entice him further. Maybe she'll try to stick out her tongue, but that won't make any difference either. Like it or not, she belongs to this man. And she wouldn't have any other way.

He kisses her, he teases her, and he continues to work her. Every moment sends another wave of anticipatory ecstasy through her body. She can't really breathe, and she definitely can't think. At moments like this, she can only close her eyes and the savor those powerful pulses.

"You belong to me," he says again. Those words are completely true.

She swallows, and she feels the collar around her neck. He works her hard and fast. He shows her just what she is: a sex slave, a horny bimbo.

"Tell me you're grateful."

"I'm, I'm so grateful, master! Thank you for using me! Thank you for using my body! I'm, I'm so grateful! I love being your bimbo. I love being your slave! Thank you, thank you, thank you!"

And she is gushing like some silly airhead, but she can't stop herself. This is what her Master expects from her, and this is what she will give him.

Willingly.

Eagerly.

"Now you can come," he tells her, and her pussy tightens. Finally, she doesn't have to hold back and in that instant, she cries out, arching her back. She can feel him, working her. Every movement sends another burst of stimulus running through her skin. She cries out, screaming until there is nothing left in her lungs.

He's climaxing as well, his cock pulsating. He works her until he's done. Then he pulls out, and he looks down at his girl. "Such a pretty bimbo," he says. "Go get yourself cleaned up." He unlocks her from her shackles, and Sabrina scurries to obey.

Sabrina blinked.

Disoriented and confused, she didn't know what just happened. Her mouth was dry, her muscles sore intense, like she been sitting in one position for a long time. She looked down, and she felt it, that dampness right between her legs. Her skin felt hot and sticky, like she'd been sweating.

Then she realized something. The rest of her office was dark, only illuminated by the glow of her laptop. The glare was sharp, and made her eyes hurt, especially when she turned her attention from the shadows back to her bright screen.

It was dark outside. Really dark.

When she first walked into her office and opened up that email, the sun was setting...At a glance, she checked the time listed in the corner of her screen. It was almost 10:00 PM.

"No, that's not possible," she whispered. There was no way she had been sitting there for hours on end.

And yet, Sabrina started to stand, and she wobbled. She fell back into her office chair, and then she swallowed. She was thirsty, but there was something else, another instinct that vied for her attention.

When she tried to catch her breath, Sabrina realized she needed something. She needed to touch herself. Second by second, she could feel it, that yearning right there, pulsating between her legs. She was horny, so incredibly aroused.

She managed to get up onto her feet, and she yanked down her panties. She bunched them up between her knees, she sat back down, and she started to masturbate.

With one hand, she worked her breasts. With the other, she stroked her slit. Her nipples hardened, and she started to pant.

Sabrina didn't even know if the door was locked; she couldn't make herself care.

Biting down into the inside of her mouth, she kept going. It only took a few seconds. There is a burst of pleasure, the rush of ecstasy, and then she just fell back into her chair, panting while she waited for her body to calm down again.

Chapter 3

Getting out of the office proved to be somewhat stressful. She had to be quick. She worried that someone might see her, perhaps some overly eager programmer who wanted to demonstrate just how useful he could be.

Sabrina reached into her desk, and she pulled out a small hand mirror. Her skin looked clammy, her hair was messed up, and she probably reeked a little. When she got up again, she reached out for her desk, and she used to the solid wood for support.

Yes, that certainly helped. She wobbled around, almost like a baby horse learning to walk for the first time. Eventually, she straightened her back, she smoothed out her skirt, and then she grabbed her purse. She headed outside, chin up.

She did her best to pretend that nothing strange was going on.

But even as she walked out to the parking lot, Sabrina yanked out her cell phone. She brought up her email server, and she checked through the messages.

The email was still there, *I know what you want.*

Very carefully, she checked the message, and she expected to see the attachment. Out in the cold air, Sabrina stopped...The attachment wasn't there. It was no longer on the screen. She swiped her finger down and up, searching through every inch and pixel, but that word was just gone. She couldn't see the icon.

Sabrina knew a little bit about programming, and she had spent a lot of time online over the years, but she didn't think something like this was possible. What was it? Some kind of self-destructing attachment?

Someone sent this to her.

Why?

It didn't feel like some sort of attack. It was just arousing, incredibly arousing. It felt like someone reached right into her mind and triggered her deepest fantasies.

Sabrina locked her teeth together. She didn't like the idea that someone could mess with her. As she walked back to her car, she could feel the aggression start to pump through her body.

First, she decided that she was going to leave this alone. It was just a message, it was just a fantasy. Nothing important happened. As far as she knew.

Sabrina got into her car, and she stabbed the key into the ignition, and then she paused. With her hands on the steering wheel, she realized something. She had lost several hours. For all she knew, her hands had been busy all that time.

Maybe she had sent out sensitive information. Her website server contained lots of emails, phone numbers, and ISP addresses for Giggle Girl users. What if she transferred out that information? They had payroll data on their bloggers as well, a group of which numbered in the thousands.

A hundred other scenarios popped through her head. Sabrina yanked out her phone, and she logged back into her computer in her office. She started double checking the tracking software to see exactly what she had done.

Nothing.

She checked the logs. A couple of hours ago, she opened up an attachment. After that, nothing.

Apparently, Sabrina had simply sat there, fantasizing and staring at her computer screen.

And yet, someone had effectively hypnotized her.

The corners of her mouth froze up. Hypnotized? Really?

Something like that wasn't supposed to be possible. Sabrina didn't pretend to be an expert in every field, but she had a pretty good sense that people couldn't just use a couple of colors or some flashing images on a screen to provoke a psychological reaction.

Even as that dismissal sounded reasonable, Sabrina couldn't help but remember those kids whose epileptic seizures could be triggered by flashing lights. Clearly, there was a connection between the eyes and the brain, so maybe someone figured it out. Maybe someone figured out the right pattern or sequence to provoke a particular set of images.

Sabrina didn't particularly like this line of reasoning, so she made a phone call. She pulled up one name, Alexander.

The phone rang just once. "Yes?"

"Alexander, I'm forwarding you an email. I want you to track the sender. Find out everything you can."

"No problem." Dead air. He waited, still on the line. He needed to hear if there was anything else.

"Thank you," she told him, and he hung up on her.

The next morning, Sabrina went back into work. She kept checking her phone, wondering when Alexander was going to get back to her. He was one of the best security consultants on the planet.

His prices were outrageous, yet Sabrina didn't care. Someone messed with her, so now she needed to figure out who.

Her phone didn't offer up any good news. She didn't have any messages from Alexander, but as she checked the screen for the hundredth time, the small device buzzed, announcing that she had a meeting in a few minutes.

Kyle brought her some coffee, and she headed back to the conference room.

Once there, she found several more of the investment bankers. She filled her lungs, she exhaled slowly, and she shook their hands, one after another. They introduced themselves. Jack, Mike, Terrance, Cale, and Shawna. Somehow, they all looked the same to her. Even the girl seemed to somehow blend into the group.

Sabrina may have majored in business back in school, but she never really understood these people. To her, business could be fascinating because it combined so many different fields. Starting a company meant dealing with dozens of different subjects. A lot of business majors may have lacked imagination, but the really good ones understood that they needed to be open to differing perspectives.

That's why she always found it so funny when some of her fellow students complained about their general education courses. As far as they were concerned, a future CEO shouldn't have to take classes like history, English, or science.

They were idiots.

Sabrina made her way back to her meeting, and she sat toward the back once again. She crossed her arms over her chest. She knew her body language was hostile, but she didn't care.

The younger woman, Shawna, stood up, and she started her PowerPoint. She talked about how the IPO would proceed along with some potential issues.

"Are you expecting a problem?" Sabrina asked halfway through.

"Not exactly," said the girl. She had on dark rimmed glasses and a pantsuit. With her hair tied back into a braid, she looked like a little girl doing her best to pretend that she was an adult.

Sabrina did her best not to get annoyed with this girl. She was probably just some low level drone. She was probably doing her best to get through this.

"Continue," Sabrina said, although she still had her phone in her hand. She kept waiting, wondering when Alexander was going to get back to her.

The meeting came to an end, and Shawna scurried away, clearly relieved.

Sabrina got up, and she was going to head back to her office to do some real work.

"Is everything okay?" asked one of the investment bankers.

Sabrina glanced up, and she tried to remember this guy's name. Terrance popped into her head, but she couldn't be certain if that was the right answer, so she just flashed a reassuring smile. "I'm fine. Something of a rough night."

"Look, I know this sounds really intimidating, but it won't be so bad. Pretty much every executive gets nervous when an IPO starts to roll around."

"How do you think it'll go?" Sabrina asked, somewhat surprised. Then again, she reevaluated this guy. He had blonde hair. As far as she was concerned, that was a strike against him. But still, there was something articulate in the way he spoke, and he didn't have the lifeless cow eyes of so many other bankers.

"The markets have been cooperating with a lot of IPOs this year, but there's never a guarantee. Frankly, I think it mostly comes down to your numbers, and they're good. You have a solid business model, and you have a lot of good content. More to the point, you've waited a long time to go public, so it should work. You have a solid track record. That's not true for a lot of companies."

"Thanks," she said, walking away.

"Sabrina?" Terrance asked her.

"Yes?" She waited there, braced in the doorway.

"Can I buy you a drink tonight?"

Normally, she would have said no. Normally, she would have told him some excuse about how she needed to work or that it was simply inappropriate considering that he was a consultant for her company. But then, she considered the way he filled out that suit, and she nodded.

"Sure," she said. "You have my number. Text me the details."

Sabrina went back into her office, and she found something. A small brown box, wrapped and taped up neatly.

This didn't make sense. She always picked up her packages from her box in the mailroom. No one ever delivered a particular piece directly to her workspace.

An instinct niggled at the back of her mind, so she carefully approached, almost like she worried it might be a bomb. But no, that was silly. Sure, her website generated a little bit of controversy, but there were no real targets out there.

In fact, Sabrina was one of the CEOs who didn't get a death threat every once in a while. Despite her brusque personality, she couldn't even think of one employee who had been fired badly, someone who swore revenge. She rolled her eyes at the concept.

Focusing her attention on the package, Sabrina sat down.

The box didn't have an address on it. It didn't even have her name. Instead, there was just one line of text written out in black ink. *I know what you want.*

Sabrina ran her teeth along her bottom lip, wondering what this would be. Her heart started to beat a little bit more quickly, and it felt like a sugar rush. She hadn't even touched it yet, and there was still this rush of adrenaline flashing through her body.

She sat down, she reached out for the box, and then she stopped herself. No, she had to do this methodically. She had to be smart.

She pulled out her phone, she dialed up his number, and she waited. Again, the ring tone only sounded once, and then she heard his voice. "I can't find anything."

"Nothing?"

"Whoever sent you that email has done a very good job of hiding his tracks. He used a series of proxy servers. I've been able to track him across half the world, but it's slow going. I can keep at it if you like, but there is a very good chance the message will have originated from a café without any surveillance."

"Even if there wasn't surveillance, couldn't you find a witness or something?" She hated the fact that she sounded like some character from a crime procedure show, but Sabrina didn't know what else to do.

"Possibly," Alexander allowed. "However, if the Wi-Fi connection is large enough, it won't make a difference. Your sender wouldn't have needed to even be in the room. He could have been in the parking lot or in another business altogether. It's also possible that he has access to a daisy chain protocol miles away."

Sabrina exhaled through her teeth. She didn't like that kind of reasoning, but she was smart enough to know that sometimes systems could be exploited. And sometimes, they wouldn't be caught.

"Thank you," she said, lowering her phone and disconnecting. She dropped her cell back on the desk, and then she looked at the box. Her eyes kept going over the handwriting.

I know what you want. Four words. They sounded so simple. They seemed so innocuous, yet full of potential.

Sabrina understood exactly what she should do. She should just take this box and go throw it in the trash. If someone was messing with her, she didn't need to cooperate. She didn't have to play along. And yet, she kept thinking about that fantasy, about those images that swirled and spun through her head.

Even now, she could pull back just this little taste of arousal, and she wanted more.

Sabrina grabbed her scissors, and she cut through the tape. She opened the box, and she found two items inside, protected by a flurry of Styrofoam.

First, there was a flash drive. It looked so small and innocuous. Next, she found a metal circlet.

"What is this?" Sabrina whispered.

Her phone started buzzing for her attention. Sabrina grabbed it, and she answered. "What's going on?"

"You have another meeting in a few minutes," Kyle told her.

Sabrina picked up the circlet. It looked so delicate, but she could feel the hefty weight. Again, she mouthed this question, "What are you?"

"Hello? Sabrina, are you there? What you want me to tell the consultants?"

"Tell them I'll be there," Sabrina replied, but she grabbed her laptop and the flash drive.

This is going to be another long, excruciatingly boring meeting involving the consultants, her management team, and some of the company's major investors. At this point, the investors were practically jubilant. They were about to cash out and get their long-awaited returns.

Sabrina was grateful for all of the support she received from those individuals, but at this point, she couldn't help but recall one simple fact. They did this for the money. They weren't interested in helping society or pushing the bounds of technology.

Then again, these were the people who just looked at the numbers.

Perhaps there were investors out there who really wanted to improve humanity. If so, these weren't them.

She sat in the back, she had her laptop, and she opened it up. She plugged in the flash drive, and she waited, expecting something the pop up. Her heart kicked in her chest, especially when she wondered if those colors were going to reappear.

But now, nothing happened. There wasn't even the usual announcement telling her that new hardware had been detected.

She double checked the directories, and then she saw it, the flash drive.

At a moment like this, Sabrina knew that she was supposed to be focused on the presenter. Their information probably wasn't important, but maybe they would surprise her this time around.

Sabrina glared at her computer, almost like she expected it to provide some feedback, perhaps helpful advice. It didn't. So after a few more seconds, she double tapped on that icon, and then two files appeared.

The first would run some kind of program.

The other was a simple text document.

Sabrina decided to be conservative; she tapped on the document, opening it up. The first page was a series of hyperlinks. They appeared to be organized under two main headings: *Technical Specifications* and *Programming.*

Because she wanted to know exactly what she was dealing with, she chose the specifications first. Another page of text appeared, this one filled with images of the circlet from before.

Except it wasn't just a circular piece of metal. No, it was something else entirely.

It was a collar.

Sabrina wasn't an electrical engineer by any measure, but she had learned a bit about computers, so she knew how different circuits could interact. Or to the point, these technical specifications seemed to have been written for an amateur. The more she read, the more she came to the conclusion that this wasn't designed for an actual engineer.

The collar was actually pretty amazing. The more she studied it, the more impressed she became.

It had a series of controllers, dozens of buffers, and an incredibly powerful microprocessor. At the base, there was even one item that made her think this had to be a joke.

According to the specifications, this collar came with an MRI machine. More than anything, Sabrina really wished she had brought the collar with her into the meeting. She wanted to examine it, to make sure that this wasn't some kind of elaborate prank or an insane delusion.

The more she considered how everything fit together, the more she came to one conclusion. It made sense.

Sabrina inhaled and exhaled. On the other side of the conference room, the presenter kept going. She was talking about public perceptions or something, but the CEO in the room really didn't care.

Instead, she was looking at the electrodes. The collar could be used to track blood flow in the brain to make rudimentary readings. If certain conditions were met, then the subject wearing the collar could be punished.

Sabrina felt the crimson heat of blush spring along her face. She was turning red. Her heart started to thunder much more quickly in her chest, the staccato rhythm beating into her ribs.

It felt like she was running, like she was sprinting away from some monster. So she minimized the image, and she looked back at the presenter. She needed several more minutes to get her body under control.

Her body did begin to relax, for the most part, but Sabrina kept itching to open up her computer again. She wanted to see the item. She wanted to examine and explore it more.

This was stupid. Again and again, she tried to tell herself that. Those thoughts were supposed to ameliorate this desire. She was playing with fire. Someone built this machine, and they sent it to her.

Why?

They know about me. They know what I want, Sabrina realized. She was a rich woman. She shouldn't be messing around with something like this. Mouth dry, she kept thinking about the logical thing to do. She just had to take the collar and the flash drive, and she had to throw them away. It wouldn't be difficult.

And yet, she wasn't going to do that.

Sabrina knew herself well enough. She was intrigued, and she wouldn't be able to discard this discovery. So instead, she sat through the meeting. She sat through the meeting, and she realized something. Not only was her skin hot, but her slit was dampening as well.

Some time ago, she tried to take a yoga class. Her teacher taught meditation, and he focused on the idea of imagining one's troubles or worries or stress as a ball. Take that ball, turn it into an object, and you can let it go. You could release it, and that was supposed to help her.

Even though Sabrina didn't really appreciate the supposed spirituality of yoga classes, she nonetheless used that same strategy. She concentrated on her arousal, and she did her best to let it go. That seemed to help for a few seconds, but there was just this impulse at the back of her mind, this yearning. Sabrina wanted to read the rest of the document. She wanted to study the specifications.

She wanted to pick up the collar, to slide it around her neck.

No!

Giving in, she opened up her computer, and the presenter didn't even seem to notice. Sabrina went back to the technical details, and she realized something. Aside from the batteries and microprocessors, the MRI, and the controllers, this collar also came with quite a bit of data storage. She didn't understand why. There were also microphones and several camera lenses. She didn't remember seeing those.

"Did you have a question?" asked the presenter.

Sabrina glanced up without missing a beat. "No, I'm good," she said, and she went back to her schematics.

The presenter just shrugged and continued droning on from one PowerPoint slide to the next. Exhaling through her mouth, Sabrina sucked on her bottom lip for a few more seconds. That's when she noticed something else.

The collar had a set of electromagnets.

Locks.

This collar was intense. It was serious.

"Are there any other questions?" asked the presenter. That's when Sabrina closed her laptop, and she marched out of the room. She practically broke into a sprint as her shoes touched to the hallway floor.

Kyle was waiting for her outside of her office. He probably had something he wanted to say to her.

"Hold all of my calls, and cancel all of my meetings. Not to be disturbed."

He opened his mouth for a moment. There is obviously something he meant to say, but then he realized his boss wasn't going to be distracted. "I understand," he told her just as she shut and locked her door.

Sabrina thought she might do this at home, but she didn't want to wait. Impatience itched at the back of her neck. But she opened up her laptop, and she reviewed the data again. She had a good sense of what this device could do.

So she checked out the programming options. She went through the pages, one after another.

The device was very simple. It operated on a punishment system. Rewards, apparently, could be offered out by the controller. The collar, on the other hand, could deliver one electrical shock after another. The system operated by numbers, one through ten. One would be a small shock. Ten would be intensely painful.

She read those words several more times, and she considered the power they would give to another individual.

Of course, Sabrina had read fantasies about shock collars. In fact, she had even gone online and watched people mess around with them. It all seemed so silly to her, and yet those images were arousing as well.

The idea of surrendering control, of being punished, it all triggered something inside of her, this instinct that didn't make any sense.

Yet Sabrina didn't really care either. She had to do this.

Yes, she was messing with fire. Yes, she was doing something dangerous. Yes, this could go so horribly wrong, but she couldn't focus on those realities. Instead, she kept reading and reading.

She learned all about this device.

And when she was done, she went back to the start program.
She double clicked. She ran the executable.

For three full seconds, nothing happened. Then her screen went black, and white text began to stream down her monitor. Sabrina watched, entranced.
Finally, a series of menus appeared. Most of them were currently grayed out. There was a box at the top.
Begin programming.
Sabrina reached for the touchpad of her laptop, and she clicked on the box.
Set Timer became available.
Exhaling a slow breath, she clicked, and then the numbers appeared. Apparently, she could set this for just a few seconds, a few minutes, hours or even days. She decided to do something simple.
Sixty seconds.
Confirm parameters? Appeared on her screen along with yes and no options.
Sabrina clicked on yes.
The collar snapped closed.
Tentatively, like she thought it might be some sort of snake or poisonous animal, Sabrina reached out, and she picked up the piece of hardware. Before, the circlet had been slightly open. There was a smooth hinge along the back, right next to the MRI.
Holding the device, Sabrina pulled gently, almost expecting the piece to open up again. It didn't. It remained locked shut, and when she glanced back at the program on her laptop, she saw the timer running down in the bottom right-hand corner of the screen.
9...8...7...
Sabrina held onto the device like it was a wild animal. She kept watching, waiting. She didn't have any thoughts, yet her eyes remained pinned onto this shining, almost silver device.
...1
The collar snapped open again.

Gripping the device in one hand, she contemplated what she was going to do next.

"This is insane," she said quietly.

Somehow, the sound of her own voice wasn't enough to dissuade her. She went back to the menu, and she changed of the timer to three minutes. She slipped the metal around her neck, and then she covered the arrow above the button.

She entered the data. Another question popped up.

Confirm parameters?

Holding onto the collar with one hand, her finger braced on the mouse. Again and again, Sabrina told herself that she shouldn't do this. What if something went wrong? What if the collar was too tight? For all she knew, this thing would start choking her.

In a best case scenario, she would be able to rush back out into the hallway, and someone would come help her. Someone would cut her out of this thing, but there would be questions, so many embarrassing questions.

If things went really wrong, it could choke her.

Realizing this, Sabrina hit the button anyway. She knew she was playing with fire; she was screwing around with a deep-seated fantasy, but she couldn't help herself either.

The electromagnets activated, locking the collar around her neck. The metal tips came together, snapping in place.

For a few seconds, the brain didn't do anything at all. She sat there, and she didn't twitch a single muscle.

Then, tentatively, she reached up for the collar, and she tried to pull the magnetized edges apart.

She worked at it for less than a second when a spark of electricity jumped through the collar into her skin. She let out a quick yelp, practically squealing. Her eyes watered, and she stumbled back into her seat. She moved with enough force to make her chair roll back into the wall.

Panting, Sabrina wanted to try to grab at the collar again, but she stopped at the last second. As the pain faded, she glanced back at the screen.

A new dialog box had appeared. *Subject has attempted to remove the collar. Disciplinary Protocol 1 has been initiated. Repeat?*

Really quickly, she clicked on the no button. Sabrina didn't think she could take another burst of pain like that.

Instead, she got up, she crossed of the room, and she went over into the small bathroom connected to her workspace. She looked at herself in the mirror, and she saw it, the collar right there.

"Sabrina? Are you okay?" Someone was knocking at the door to her office. It was Kyle.

"I'm fine," she called back to him.

"Are you sure? I thought I heard something," he told her.

Blushing brightly, she cleared her throat. She did her best to sound perfectly calm and confident. "I'm fine," she repeated. "Sorry if I scared you."

"Is there anything I can get you?"

Sabrina glanced back at her reflection. She was stuck in this collar. If anyone saw her, they would know something was going on. That thought sent another thrill running down between her legs. She could feel the tension in her slit.

"I'm fine. Just get back to work," she told him.

"Understood," he replied.

Once he was gone, Sabrina went back to her desk, and she watched the screen. The numbers counted down. *02:09...02:08...02:07...*

In the next couple of minutes, Sabrina just watched those digits. Finally, it hit zero, and the collar popped back open.

If Sabrina could have controlled herself, she would have taken off the collar, she would've stuffed into the box, and she would have thrown it away. Someone sent this to her. Someone smart or rich. She didn't know how much money it would take to develop this sort of technology. It had a miniature MRI built into it, for crying out loud.

It was built for behavioral modification. Whoever did this understood psychology, electronics, and something else...They knew something about her.

Unlike so many other people, Sabrina never felt compelled to share her deepest secrets with anyone else. Even in college, when she occasionally dated, she remained mostly closed off. She might fool around with one guy or another, yet she never developed the kind of intimacy that so many of her female friends loved to gush about.

No one knew about her predilections.

At least, she didn't think anyone knew about her secret desires.

Sabrina went back to the text document, and she scanned it more closely this time. That's when she realized that there was another section, one she had missed before.

Crinkling her brows, she wondered how she made this sort of mistake. She parted her lips, and she focused on one simple fact. When it came to this collar and that emailed attachment, Sabrina didn't know how to think clearly. Time and time again, she proved that.

This new section of text focused on training scenarios.

The MRI machine couldn't read exact thoughts, but it could track how the brain related to particular concepts. For example, this device could be used to train the wearer to stop thinking about self identification.

Every time Sabrina used her own name, even silently, it lit up a certain part of her cerebral cortex. This device could read that pattern, and it could punish her.

Similarly, when she began to become aroused, the collar could detect it and punish her. If she thought about any of her fantasies, it could do the exact same thing. In short, this device could be used for psychological training.

Tilting her head to the side, she kept reading, and she realized something else. The pain could be used in a much more extensive way. Electrified prongs could be activated if the wearer stopped thinking about something in particular.

Sabrina couldn't help herself; she decided to experiment again. Holding the collar up to her neck, she copied a set of instructions from the text, and she copied it into the executable file.

Her shoulders rose and fell.

She was very careful to change the timer this time.
01:00.
The timer started, and she focused on the screen. She did her best to keep her thoughts blank.

This isn't so hard, Sabrina thought to herself. *I can totally do this!*

Just as a thought finished, a stab electricity shot into her skin, making her yelp all over again. Her hand flew up, and she touched her palm to her mouth.

"Sabrina? Are you sure you're okay?" Kyle asked her again, this time without bothering to knock. At least he stayed on his side of the door.

I was smart to lock it, Sabrina thought. A second burst of electricity flashed through her skin, flaring down and throughout her nervous system. This time, she whimpered into her hand, and her eyes watered, but she didn't think he could hear her.

Pulling her hand away, Sabrina had to say something. "I'm fine!" This time, her voice shook. She couldn't sound aggressive. She could just tell him to go away.

The instructions had been very clear. If she felt even a hint of accomplishment, then the collar would punish her.

"I can come in there," he told her through the door. "If you need me to, I can call a doctor or something." He sounded really uncertain.

"I'm fine. It's okay."

He disappeared, and then the timer hit zero. The collar snapped open, and she pulled it off. When she dropped it onto her desk, Sabrina sat in her chair. She stared up at the ceiling even as she panted, thinking about what she had just done. This thing basically read her mind, and it punished her for behaving like an executive.

That's when she realized she was horny, desperately so.

The arousal played along every inch of her skin. Now that she didn't have the collar wrapped around her neck, Sabrina stood up, she pulled down her panties, and she hitched up her skirt. Before she knew it, she was stroking herself, rubbing to fingers along her crevice.

Her heart started to beat more quickly, heat expanded along the contours of her limbs and down her chest. She came closer and closer to an orgasm. And then, the pleasure eclipsed all of her thoughts. She stopped clinging to any ideas as those sensations pummeled into her.

She didn't whimper or cry out. She opened her mouth, and she panted until the pleasure finally started to dissipate. That's when she knew what she had to do.

Chapter 4

She rushed out of the office without saying a word to anyone. Of course, Kyle saw her go, and he lifted his head. He tried to call out to her, but she ignored him. She had the box hidden away in her purse.

With every step, she wondered what she was going to do next. She didn't have a plan. She didn't have a strategy. She just knew that she had to act. Her footsteps clicked against the asphalt as she made her way back to her car.

She drove home, quickly. She locked her vehicle, and she rushed back up to the steps of her house. Once inside, she locked the door, almost like she worried someone might pursue her.

Sabrina didn't know where she should go next.

Her office.

Like so many other executives, Sabrina did a lot of work at home. She answered emails, she handled some of the simple programming tasks, and she considered dozens of proposals on a weekly basis. Today, she went into her office, and she plugged in the flash drive. She brought up the program connected to the collar, and she took out the device itself.

She set it down on her desktop, and she stared at it for almost an entire minute.

Tensing her lips, Sabrina went through the text again. She focused on that one section. It had the commands for behavior modification. Her heart started to beat more quickly, boom, boom, boom through every second.

She picked up the collar, and she decided to try something else.

There.

A simple set of commands but she copied them and pasted them into the actual program. Then she pulled the collar back up and around her neck. She set the timer.

Confirm parameters?

She got brave (or foolish), and she pushed the yes button.

The collar snapped shut. Just a little bit tight against her throat, it was impossible to ignore.

02:00...01:59...01:58...

Her hand immediately flew up to her hair, and she started to twirl those strands around fingertip. "Hi! My name is Sabrina, and I'm just a silly girl." Those words left her mouth, and she instantly felt foolish. "This is dumb. What am I..."

Before she could finish the question, another burst of electricity flashed through her skin. Uncompromising and totally merciless, the collar delivered a painful jolt. Agony exploded through her skin, she fell back against her chair's pad.

Eyes wet, she started to twirl her fingers through her hair once again. "My name is Sabrina! I'm a silly! I don't like to think for myself!" Her eyes drifted down to the timer. Apparently, that behavior wasn't forbidden. But for the next minute and a half, she had to be good. If she stopped thinking like a bimbo, she would be punished. It would be painful, and there would be trouble.

"I want to be a cheerleader! I love it when guys watch me. I want to dance around. Oh, tonight, I really want to go to a club. It would feel so good to dance around, and I'd have so much fun!" She started giggling like some blonde airhead.

That gave her another idea. But it was dumb.

The collar shocked her again, sending another barrage of hot electricity through her skin. She let out a yelp. Panting once, then twice, she started to speak again. "I want to be the horny dumb girl, the one who will do anything to get laid. That's who I am. I'm just a silly girl. I don't have any good ideas. I need, I need a man to tell what to think!"

She glanced back at the counter. She still had more than a minute.

Sabrina inhaled, and she knew she had to keep going. But she couldn't think of anything, so the collar punished her. Electricity stabbed into her skin, lighting up the pain receptors throughout her body. She fell forward, on her knees.

"I need to be a slave. I need to be property. If I had a man to tell me what to do, then I would always be a good girl!" Even though her eyes were watering, she giggled. More importantly, she meant it.

In that moment, she knew her place, just as she knew exactly where she belonged.

"I want to be a bimbo. I want to have a boyfriend or husband who can tell me what to do. He'll be, he'll be so smart, smarter than me! He'll talk about all the things he's done, and I'll just blink along and nod and tell him he's so smart! I'll tell him that I'm so impressed because he'll be so intellectual and everything!"

The collar finally popped open. Sabrina pulled it off, and she slammed it back down on her desk.

Less than a second later, she had her hand between her legs. She slid her other fingers up her blouse, and she started to touch her nipples. She pinched and pulled. At the same time Sabrina stroked and caressed her pussy. She rubbed herself through the layer of her panties.

The orgasm washed through her, crashing down like this powerful wave. It was a tsunami, and when it was done, she sat there at her desk, exhausted and spent.

Forcing herself back up, Sabrina knew she needed to do. She grabbed her phone, and she pulled up his number.

"Sabrina Riley's office," Kyle answered after just a couple of rings.

"Kyle, would you like to go out tonight? I need to blow off some steam. Maybe you could help me," she said. She did her best to sound normal, like nothing special had happened, and yet there was that frantic edge in her voice.

She had no way of knowing whether or not, Kyle heard it.

"I'd love that," he told her.

"Pick me up at seven," she told him, and she pulled the phone away from her ear, clicking it off without waiting for any sort of confirmation.

Sabrina headed back into her bedroom. She practically stumbled into the bathroom. She pulled off her blouse and her skirt. She discarded her panties and her socks in the span of a couple of heartbeats. She turned on the water, and she waited just long enough for it to become tepid. Then she stepped under those jets of liquid, and she let the water wash the salt and grime from her body.

After today, she felt dirty, used.

On more than one occasion, Sabrina had fantasized about becoming a sex slave, an object to be used by her Master. Even now, she closed her eyes, and she tried to think of his face, his name. Someone sent her that collar and the email. Someone was messing with her.

She almost had an idea of who it could be.

He needed to be smart, he needed resources, and most importantly, he had to know about her interests and tastes.

She had someone in mind. Perhaps she would be able to test him at some point. Yes, that sounded like such a good idea.

Sabrina slowly made her plans. Every thought and idea seemed to trudge sluggishly through her brain. And yet, even in the shower, she found herself pulling the head away from its perch above her. She took the jets of water, and she aimed them down along her body. She twirled the showerhead through the air, teasing her breasts first. Then she drifted lower, lower, lower until that delicious pressure was right there between her inner thighs. The hot water made it so easy.

She climaxed again.

After that, Sabrina knew that she had to take a nap. She finished washing, she turned off the jets, and she dried off. The coarse towel felt good against her skin. But once she wasn't dripping, Sabrina retreated back into the bedroom. She fell down onto her back, and she contemplated the possibility.

What if it was really him? What if her guess was correct?

Sabrina knew that she shouldn't judge. Seriously, she considered her own fantasies, and she laughed. Magazines and feminists alike tried to chase her down, hoping that she would offer some little bit of wisdom or something interesting to say about her success.

In the end, there was only one conclusion she could draw. For all of this time, she had worked, pounding through her studies and the competition, only to realize something.

She didn't care.

There she was, on the cusp of her first IPO, and she didn't hunger for more. She wasn't interested in considering just how much she might make on that first day.

No, she was bored. She suffered from ennui. There was this malaise deep within her psyche. The exact wording didn't matter because she knew the truth. She wasn't happy. And then a smile tugged at her lips because she considered how it would feel to have that metal band around her neck, this symbol of her subservience and her subjugation.

For a long time, she relaxed on the sheets. Even after the last bits of moisture dried away from her body, and even after she got cold, Sabrina just relaxed. She felt the weight of her body, and she allowed herself to recharge.

Sabrina couldn't rest forever. She had a date.

She decided to go sexy. She pillaged through her closet, considering all of the different options. Considering her profession, she routinely had to go hang out with wealthy investors, men and women who'd expect her to pull on a sexy dress and some high heels.

It only took a few moments of consideration for her to pick red. This dress was tight, it squeezed on her breasts, and it highlighted the best curves along her legs and ass. She pulled on a pair of matching heels, and when she was done, she topped it all off with some crimson lipstick.

From there, she did her hair. One French braid.

Taken together, she checked out her appearance, and she was more than satisfied. She looked hot, dangerous. More to the point, she carried herself like a girl who wanted to get laid.

Flirtatious, she winked at her reflection. That's when the doorbell rang, and Sabrina headed out to greet her date.

Unsurprisingly, Kyle looked good, and cute. He had his hair slicked back, and he smiled at her. He was clean shaven, and the aroma of his cologne definitely triggered something inside of her.

"You look incredible," he said, clearly doing his best not to sound overly impressed. He succeeded. Mostly.

Kyle held out his arm like a gentleman, and she took it. He escorted her back to his car, and he even opened the door for her. Perhaps this is going to work out nicely after all, Sabrina reflected.

On their way to the restaurant, they chatted. He didn't bring up work, and neither did she. In fact, this made it surprisingly easy to pretend that there wasn't any kind of professional relationship between them.

Every once in a while, Sabrina would just glance over at this man, and she wouldn't see him as her assistant or subordinate. No, she simply viewed him as a prime example of the male species. He looked good with that strong jaw, his muscled shoulders, and his big hands.

Just that afternoon, Sabrina had taken this boy, commanding him to drop to his knees. He had obeyed. But what if there was more to Kyle that she first suspected? What if he had done something unique?"

Her body quivered at the prospect.

They were seated quickly at the restaurant. They sat together in a booth, and Sabrina actually scooted closer and closer.

At one point, Kyle actually pretended to yawn, stretching his arms into the air before resting it on her shoulder. She giggled like a schoolgirl, very pleased with this. Under normal circumstances, the sort of game might have seemed asinine. But right then and right there, she found it exciting.

They ordered, and they kept eating. They kept flirting.

But after the server brought them their wine, Sabrina glanced back at this man. "Kyle, I got an interesting package today."

"Really?" He had his eyes on her, yet his tone betrayed one fact. He didn't care. He had no interest in what she received. On the contrary, this man simply wanted to unwrap her. He wanted to strip her out of that dress, to push her down onto the bed, to hold her hand to claim her.

It was primal and simple. It was irresistible.

"Yes. It was a very interesting package. You wouldn't know anything about it, would you?"

This time, he raised an eyebrow. "No, why would I?"

Sabrina pressed her lips together, doing her best to suppress the disappointment. But she still couldn't be sure. Perhaps this was part of the game. "Tell me about your ideal relationship."

"My ideal relationship or my ideal girl?" He smirked back at her, and she could tell that he was trying to be confident, but there something off. He glanced over her shoulder, like she intimidated him.

"Ideal girl."

"Well, she's got to be smart..." And he kept talking, but Sabrina stopped listening. His words faded away, turning into a sort of white noise.

It wasn't him.

She blinked a couple of times, doing her best to paste on an interested façade, but it was difficult. She had been almost certain, thinking that it was Kyle. When she reflected on his expertise, it made sense. He had a background in engineering. He obviously spent a lot of time with her, so it would have made sense if he accidentally stumbled on one of her fantasy books.

...It would have been so perfect. She loved the idea of losing control to her assistant. Maybe he would have even been resentful, thinking of the many times had been forced to fetch her coffee. But now, he would take control. He would be the Master, and he would make her pay for every indignity, every professional slight.

He would spank her, tease her, humiliate her. There'd be nothing she could do because he locked a collar around her neck...

Hot and wet, Sabrina couldn't just sit there in the restaurant anymore.

All of a sudden, she looked around the rest of the room. "You want to get out of here?"

"Yes," he said.

"This is only going to go one way," she said, giving him one more chance.

Silently, she stared back at her assistant, hoping that he would show her exactly what he could do. He could stand up, he could take her hand, and he could laugh in her face. Or maybe he would just cup her cheek with his palm, and he could shake his head. He could tell her no. No, he wasn't going to be used again. No, he was better than that, and he was going to enjoy using her body.

Instead, he slid out of the booth, and he bowed his head down. He looked like an obedient little dog. So she couldn't respect him.

Back in her bedroom, Sabrina kicked off her shoes, she pulled down her panties, and she relaxed on her queen sized bed. She spread her legs, and there was Kyle, crawling toward her. He dipped his head down, and he kissed her inner thighs. He brushed his lips along her skin, and some part of her responded, sure.

She peeked back at him, especially as he started to lick her.

His head bobbed up and down as he swiped his tongue over her crevice. She relaxed, enjoying the soft, warm solidity of his appendage right there between her inner thighs. He pulled back for a moment, perhaps hoping to hear her groan or moan. Instead, she remained quiet, content as he started to kiss her legs.

After a little while, he started licking her again. He pressed and the tip of his tongue right between her pussy lips. She inhaled slowly, enjoying those impulses. It felt good to have this guy down there, licking her like this. She especially enjoyed the fact that she really didn't need to reciprocate.

He wanted to please her. He wanted to show her that she was in charge.

And that's exactly what he did.

But it didn't excite her. It didn't make her quiver with ecstasy.

Sabrina didn't know what to do, so she closed her eyes, and she relaxed to those sensations. She started to think of Kyle more like a vibrator or some other inanimate object. As he licked her, she allowed her thoughts to drift.

Invariably, they went in one direction.

She's tied down to her bed, her arms and legs spread. Her red dress is down on the floor, cut up into little pieces. Her panties have been ripped, and her bra has been shredded.

And there he is, her Master, the man who is about to own her. He's going to claim her, but it's going to involve so much more than simply fucking her. Yes, that would be enough to demonstrate his possession of her body, yet he craves more than that.

This man intends to possess her spirit, her willpower, and her dignity. She's going to become his grateful little toy, a sex slave dedicated and determined to please her Master at all times.

She won't think about anything else; she won't worry about anything else.

"No," she says, looking up at him with big, wide, nervous eyes. "You, you don't need to use that."

"The fact that you're trying to tell me what I should and shouldn't do means that I do," he reminds her, holding up the metal collar.

Sabrina shivers as he slides it around her neck. The electromagnets snap into place, binding the collar around her neck. It's there and there's nothing she could do about this device now.

"What, what you want me to do, Master?"

"Obey."

That's one of the parameters he can set. He can simply order her to do as she's told. After all, every time she hears a command, it triggers something inside of her brain. Other women might receive an order and bristle. Not Sabrina. When she hears the voice of her Master, and when he commands her, it lights up something. The MRI can detect it. And if she doesn't obey just an instant later, she will be punished.

"How would you like me to obey, Master?" *She grimaces at that last word.*

Perhaps she has fantasized about this, but Sabrina has been raised in a culture where women fight for respect. They try so hard to compete with the men in their lives. But here she is, naked and tied down, helpless as she addresses a man as her owner.

The metallic chill sends little shivers through her body. Bumps appear along her shoulders and down her flanks.

"Are you getting cold, slave?"

"Don't call me that," she mumbles before she really thinks about the words leaving her lips.

Electricity zaps through her body, this sharp jab of pain. She whimpers and twists, attempting to escape the restraints holding her to the bed, but there is nowhere for this girl to go. She is underneath her master, and she won't be able to get away, not until he decides to release her.

Only if he decides to release her...

"I can call you whatever I want," he tells her. "Say it."

This time, Sabrina doesn't hesitate. She can't take another shot of electricity. It hurts too much! "You can call me whatever you want."

"I'm in charge." He leans forward, and his lips are so close to her mouth. "Say it."

Sabrina desperately wants for her Master to kiss her. She wants him to press his mouth against hers. More than anything, this girl needs to surrender to those sensations.

"You're in charge."

"And you're just a silly girl. You should be grateful that you have an owner who will tell you what to do. Isn't that right?"

She nods her head down and up. The collar disciplines her again. Her Master already told her to obey. Apparently, that applies even when she isn't given a direct command. Her eyes widen at the revelation. This isn't fair!

Fairness doesn't enter into the equation, however, because she is naked and little more than a piece of property. "Yes, Master! That's right!"

This time, he kisses her, pressing his body down into hers. He is still fully clothed, but she is naked. Clothing represents status, so she becomes a plaything. She's a toy, and her Master definitely wants to enjoy himself.

His hands roam along her body, exploring her flanks, her thighs, and her breasts. He pinches her nipples, twisting them gently. Even as he kisses her, he chuckles, enjoying the little squeaks she makes.

"Good slave," he tells her, right before he bites down on her bottom lip. It's almost painful enough to make her cry out again, but then he starts kissing her some more.

Sabrina yields. She gives up everything to this man because he is her Master. His hands play along her nipples, and she arches her back. But then, he kisses her neck, and she whimpers some more. "Thank you, Master!"

He pulls back, he looks down into her brown eyes. They are so big and so innocent.

"For what?"

Sabrina doesn't want to say it, but the choice longer belongs to her. She must. She has to be a good girl, especially now that he's asked her a question.

"Thank you for making me your bimbo."

"Say it again."

He knows. He knows how those words cut down into her ego, robbing Sabrina of her independence. Even if she wants to give it up, some part of her clings to the idea that she should be independent and strong willed, intelligent and articulate.

But no, she must learn.

"Thank you for making me your bimbo, Master. I'm very, very grateful."

"Are you dumb and grateful?" The corners of his eyes crinkle with amused delight. He's having fun toying with her.

"Yes, Master," she answers, grumbling those words.

"Good." He kisses her again, only his hand snakes back between her legs. Sabrina's feet are tied to the corners of the bed, so there's nothing she can do to defend herself. His fingers probe her, exploring her. He kisses her for several more seconds, and then he pulls back. He looks down into her eyes. Her bottom lip is shaking. Her lips are wrinkled together, but she can't stop this. Her eyes are big, and her face is flushed. She wants to fight. She can't.

He strokes her, teasing her, at that she lifts her hips, giving him a better position.

Sabrina can argue all she wants. She can grumble and groan, but this is what she needs.

She arches her back, and his fingertips play along her clitoris until she surrenders. A deluge of pleasure races through her body. It splashes down along her spine, along her shoulders, over every inch. It pulsates, radiating from between her legs.

"Are you ready for me?"

"Yes, Master! Always, Master!"

"What are you again?"

"I'm your bimbo!" Sabrina chirps.

And this time, there's a big, silly smile on her face. Her eyes are so big and so sweet.

"And?"

For just a fraction of a second, she doesn't know what she's supposed to say. Then she remembers, an instant before the collar can punish her. "I'm dumb and grateful!"

"Yes, you are," he says. He sits up right between her legs, and he lowers his fly. He isn't going to strip out of his clothing. No, her Master is just going to take out his cock, and then he's going to ride her. He will be fully dressed through all of this because he gets to be a person, while she is allowed to be his bimbo slave.

He comes up to her, and he teases her with the tip of his shaft. He doesn't penetrate her, not right away. Instead, her Master forces her to wait. He makes her wiggle and squirm through the desires pounding into her body.

It feels like every nerve in her body is singing for attention. Every inch of her skin wants his touch. But he isn't giving it to her, not yet. He's going to make her wait. He's going to make her truly desperate.

"Please, please Master! I can't, I can't take it anymore!"

"Good," he says, and he kisses her again. She whimpers. She cries out, her chest vibrating through those sounds, but her Master doesn't stop.

No, he isn't done playing with his girl. This bimbo needs to learn that she has to wait until he's ready to use her, until he's ready to take her.

Finally, he pushes forward, thrusting his cock into her wet, hot, slick little opening. He pushes all the way in, burying his member deep in her body. Then he stops, he pulls back. He looks down into her eyes.

She blinks several times, feeling silly and stupid.

Sabrina can't think.

At some point in her life, she used to be an intelligent, respected young woman. Now she is just a toy, and she loves it.

He pushes forward and pulls back, giving her one thrust after another. Sabrina enjoys every moment of it. She's grateful, so incredibly grateful.

He works her harder and faster. "May I, may I have an orgasm?"

"Yes," he answers, his breath finally turning ragged.

His heart must be pounding, and he's on the verge of losing it.

He works her harder and faster, pumping, thrusting, showing her what he can do. And just then, she closes her eyes, she presses her shoulder blades back into the mattress, and she shudders through the pleasure. The explosion is a supernova, hot, incandescent, and utterly undeniable. It races throughout her body, robbing her of every modicum of control.

She can feel it, the pulsating of his shaft, working in concert with her body. He works her, going faster and faster until he's finally done. He pulls back, and he looks down at his little bimbo slave. "Well done."

Nothing could make her happier.

The last reverberations of her orgasm rippled through her body, and Sabrina opened her eyes. She looked down to see her assistant.

"Stop," she commanded, close to breathless.

At once, he pulled back, and she smiled at him. "That was very nicely done, Kyle. You can go now."

"I'm always happy to be of service," he said, standing and giving her a little bow.

Yes, she could be very pleased with his service, but it wasn't what she actually craved. He left the room. A few seconds later, she could hear his car engine start up. He was leaving. He'd probably go home and touch himself, but Sabrina didn't worry about that.

Instead, she pushed herself back up onto her feet, and she made her way into her office. She turned on the lights, and there it was, the collar sitting on the desktop, just waiting.

Sabrina turned on her computer, and she made a decision. Rather than go to the program for the collar, she opened up her email. She saw the message from before, the one from the mysterious sender.

There was the subject line, just as easy and simple as before, though the attachment remained noticeably absent.

I know what you want.

"Yes, you do," she agreed.

Sabrina hit the reply button. She started to type.

Was this a gift? She sent the message, and she waited.

Nothing happened.

And yet, she had the instinct that whoever did this would be paying attention. He would get her message, so maybe she needed to try something else. Her mouth went dry as she opened up the message and hit reply again.

Her heart started to beat more quickly as she rested her fingertips on the keys. She waited several more seconds, wondering if common sense was going to kick in. But no, Sabrina couldn't quite help herself, not this time.

Thank you, Master.

She kept staring at the screen after that. She studied those three words, wondering if she should send them. She didn't know who might receive them. And yet, this man clearly knew exactly what it took to get into her head, to get into her fantasies.

She tapped a button. The message was sent. Those electrons sped through wires, back toward their destination, wherever that happened to be.

Nostrils flared, Sabrina sat there, waiting.

BUZZ!...BUZZ!...

She jumped, startled. Sabrina glanced back at the corner of her desk, only to see her phone. She grabbed it, and she picked it up, expecting to see the number of one of the consultants or maybe an employee.

Someone probably had some technical glitch.

Unknown number.

She swiped her finger across the screen, only to realize that it wasn't a phone call. No, it was a text message.

Meet me at Donnely's. 5:00 PM.

Sabrina stared down at the screen, not sure what she should do. Just as she tried to formulate a response, a second message came through.

Wear something appropriate for a bimbo.

Just then, Sabrina realized he wasn't going to answer. She set down her phone, suddenly feeling exhausted.

She got up, and she went back to bed. She crawled under the coverlet, and she fell asleep within the span of a few seconds.

Chapter 5

Sabrina awoke, damp with sweat and slick right between her legs. In fact, before she even regained complete awareness of her surroundings, she spread her legs and she slipped her hand up her skirt. She stroked her pussy, only to remember that she didn't have on any panties. Last night, she didn't take a shower after her "date" with Kyle.

And then her eyes widened when she remembered the messages from her mysterious benefactor.

Who was he? What did he want? More importantly, what did he have planned for her?

Sabrina forced herself out of bed, and she took a shower. The water started cold, but she didn't care. By the time it heated up, she was wide awake, running through one possibility after another.

Obviously, this man wasn't a stranger. Or was that fact so obvious? It seemed possible, perhaps even probable, that he was just a hacker. This guy was obviously smart, so he could have easily made his way onto any number of her online accounts. Perhaps that's how he discovered her fetish for subservience.

Maybe she knew him.

Maybe she didn't.

Ultimately, Sabrina couldn't know for certain one way or another, not unless she decided to go out tonight.

She went back into her home office, and she sat at her desk. Dutifully, she avoided looking at the collar. Instead, she concentrated on studying her surroundings. The office wasn't especially large or even decorated. She had a couple of bookshelves with some programming manuals and a few of her favorite novels. Other than that, the room was pretty sparse.

She considered the rest of her home. The same was true there as well.

For several years now, she had focused entirely on her business. She built a company, and she could be proud of it. But what else did she have?

Sabrina didn't have any ready answers.

Nostrils flared, she got up, and she got dressed for work. She put on something appropriate, something respectable. She didn't dress like a bimbo.

Somehow, the meetings almost seemed interesting this time around. She had several more conversations with the investment bankers. They talked about how the road show was going and how some of the major institutions would react to her company.

There was even a meeting about appropriate shareholder behavior. Because she owned such a large portion of the enterprise, there were certain rules she would have to follow including a lockup. Among other things.

Sabrina nodded along. She already knew the vast majority of this information, but she had to stay focused. If she didn't, the slow tick, tick, tick of time would have driven her crazy. Seriously, Sabrina knew that she was going to leave early today.

She had to get home. She had a meeting at 5:00 PM.

Even though she did her best not to think about it, Sabrina kept checking her phone. Again and again, she checked those two text messages from the man who sent her the email and the collar.

Even as she studied those symbols in pixels on the screen of her phone, Sabrina told herself that she was doing this intelligently. Even if she put on a slightly embarrassing outfit, she was going to meet this man in a public space. If she wanted to leave, she could.

And yet, she didn't think that was going to happen. This was a man who understood her. This was a smart, powerful man. This was the kind of man who could take a girl like Sabrina and train her. He could tame her and domesticate her, breaking her will until she became utterly obedient.

Did she want that?

Some spark of desperation kept burning deep inside of her chest. Every time she thought of what might change, she felt aquiver along with cold dread.

The ambivalence seemed almost novel.

Throughout her life, Sabrina had been focused on her goals. She always knew what she wanted. At a glance, she could make any number of determinations. But not this time. This time, she kept thinking about the different possibilities, how it could go so very right or so very wrong.

And, somewhere, at the back of her mind, there is that little voice telling her that she shouldn't mess around with this. She shouldn't yield.

Perhaps it was her culture, but Sabrina kept thinking about how independence and strength were so valued by everyone she knew. Even back in middle school, all of her female friends liked to go on about how strong-willed they were. Those were the girls who would find boyfriends and could do whatever they wanted.

Sabrina wasn't so sure, especially now.

"Do you have any questions?"

This time, it was one of the bankers' lawyers talking. Apparently, he had been discussing some legal detail that Sabrina probably should have paid attention to. Then again, she already had her own a lawyer on hand to take care of this sort of detail.

"No, I'm good."

"That's all I have," he told them.

Sabrina's employees shuffled out of the room. They all wanted to get back to their desks. Like her, they tended to prefer a computer screen to a boring meeting.

The presenter finished organizing his papers. "Are you all right?"

"Distracted."

"By what?" he asked.

Sabrina looked up at him. She noticed him before, on the previous day, though she still couldn't recall his name. Apparently, he had no trouble reading her expression because he walked around the table, and he leaned forward, holding out his hand. "Cale Larsen."

"Sorry. It's good to meet you again."

"No worries. I understand that we probably all look the same to you."

She smirked slightly.

"This is going to be incredibly rude," he said, "but I would very much like to know. Did you hear anything I said?"

Normally, Sabrina didn't blush. This time, she could feel the heat curl along her cheeks. It even reached all the way up to the tips of her ears.

Before she could come up with a convincing lie, he held up his hands. "It's okay. I know that we go through all of these meetings and everything, but it's just so that you don't feel bad about giving us a cut of your IPO proceeds."

She raised an eyebrow. "Is that something you're supposed to be telling me?"

"No, probably not."

Sabrina giggled. She was surprised. She didn't think she would ever make that sort of sound. Then she remembered her fantasies, and she concentrated the man who would be meeting her at a high-end restaurant in just a few more hours.

"Tell me, Sabrina, how do you feel about social expectation?"

"Why do I get the feeling you're teasing me?"

"Because maybe I am," he replied. The lawyer leaned forward just a little bit. "But they ask a very basic question. Do you remember my name?"

She raised one corner of her mouth. She tried to summon up a name, but nothing came to her. He held out his hand again. "Allow me to introduce myself once more," he said, filling the quiet. "Cale Larsen."

"It's nice to meet you, Cale."

"You never answered my question," he said to her, shaking her hand firmly. She enjoyed the strength and solidity of his grip. Then something occurred to her.

Sabrina tilted her head to the side slightly. "Cale, what did you study in college?" There was something about this man, the way he was talking to her and flirting with her.

Could this be the man who sent her that email, who mailed her that package?

"Philosophy, mostly. Before law school, I mean."

"Philosophy? Really?" She raised one eyebrow even as she squinted back at him.

"Absolutely. Philosophy is a fantastically useful discipline for a young man to study."

"How so?" Sabrina enjoyed this conversation. If nothing else, she could use it as a distraction to hold off thoughts of the collar. She had to keep the temptation at bay. After all, part of her wanted to rush home, to put it on, to lose herself in the fantasy.

"Philosophy is all about understanding the subjective qualities of reality. You see, as near as I can tell, the world is made up of two kinds of information. Your quantitative information, data that is both numerical and verifiable. The sciences are primarily quantitative. But you also have qualities, questions of aesthetics and ethics. Those are pretty much entirely subjective."

"You don't believe in objective morality?"

"I believe that we create our own systems of belief and good behavior. Unfortunately, that extends out to the notion that there isn't a right or wrong. Instead, we do our best as people."

"So you're an optimist," she finished for him.

"I like to think I'm a realist, a realist with enough evidence to believe that people are generally good. If we weren't, I don't think society would function. But it does."

"That's a matter of opinion."

"How so?" He watched her, and it was clear that he could have answered his own question. A little thrill ran down her back. Even if this man wasn't the one who sent her that email or the package, she could at least enjoy the fact that he was attractive.

Then again, he probably had a girlfriend. If he didn't have a girlfriend, he probably had his pick of college girls hanging out at clubs. As an attorney attached to an investment bank, he probably had a very impressive bank account. Those kinds of dollars could certainly buy attention from the fairer sex.

Sabrina could have simply walked out, but she decided to play his game. "When you say society functions, you need to nail down your exact perspective. There are people out there who would say the world is breaking apart."

"True," Cale allowed, but he waved that objection away. "But then they've always been saying that. Young people have always been disrespectful and rude. Our elders have always had to walk uphill through the snow both ways to milk their cows."

Sabrina wagged her finger at him. She couldn't decide if her excitement came from the prospect of meeting her benefactor or if she actually liked flirting with this guy.

"Can you honestly tell me that there are people suffering horribly right now?"

His smirk vanished. "No, you're right. There's a great deal of suffering out in the world, and I hate to think about the various orphans and plagues that are out there. And yet, I think we're getting smarter. If you look at our technology and the way we can allocate resources, I think there's a lot of hope."

"Definitely an optimist," she said.

"Perhaps."

Sabrina felt the glow of excitement. Her cheeks were flushed.

And yet, there was still that little niggle at the back of her mind. She couldn't quite shake the disappointment. Flirting with Cale had been quite entertaining, but she couldn't alter reality. He wasn't the one.

He was flirtatious and kind. He seemed rather sweet and innocent, which surprised her even more. He was an attorney. Wasn't he supposed to be more cutthroat?

In any case, Sabrina shook off her concerns.

She had another meeting, only this one she actually wanted to attend.

She went back to her place, and she checked her text messages, almost like she worried that she had imagined them in the first place.

Back in her bedroom, she started to root through her closet. She had a variety of different outfits, but there was one in particular she intended to wear.

It was simple, just a tight black dress. The straps crisscrossed in front of her breasts, but this particular garment did a great job of highlighting her best curves and features.

When she had it on, guys couldn't quite help themselves. They had to stare, almost like their eyes became magnetized.

They followed her, and she could always feel that little thrill of power. Usually, a girl like Sabrina would get attention with what she did and what she said. But when she had on this dress with its high hem, she could get a different kind of thrill, a different kind of power.

It took her a little bit longer than she anticipated, but she found the dress. She smoothed it out, she ironed it, and she put it on along with a pair of black, silky panties and a push-up bra. After that, she checked out her reflection.

In some ways, Sabrina understood perfectly well that she looked plain. She had shining brown hair, dark eyes, and a rounded face. At best, she could look cute. But tonight, she wanted to do something more elaborate. She pinned up her hair in a curling bun. She had two bangs that looped down her forehead, just above her eyes like a pair of horns.

Like an expert, she applied her makeup. She put on eye shadow, blush, some foundation, and the requisite lipstick. When she was all done, she chose a pair of black pumps. Taken together, she looked gorgeous.

Tilting her head to the side, she held up one hand over her mouth, and she giggled.

In college, Sabrina didn't waste a lot of time at parties. But right there, in front of the mirror, she felt good. Really good. Hot. Sexy. She became the sensual girl who could seduce a guy with the right smile, the right sway of her hips.

Perhaps Sabrina could go out, even if this meeting didn't work. As she studied her reflection, she contemplated the possibility of finding some guy. She already knew that she would be able to wrap pretty much any man she wished around her little finger, especially in this tight dress.

As that possibility played up through her imagination, Sabrina waited. She anticipated some rush of tingling excitement. She didn't feel anything.

No, she wanted someone to put his hand on the back of her neck. She yearned for a collar, for a leash, for physical restraints. She wanted to blink vacantly, to know that she was just a plaything. She itched to be the silly girl who had to be told what was going on.

Sabrina needed to be a human toy. Taking control wouldn't excite her.

Once she was certain that she looked good, she went back into her office, and she collected the collar as well as the flash drive. She wasn't so foolish that she would put the device on.

Despite trepidation, she did, however, slide to the collar into her purse. After that, she swallowed once, and she got back into her car. She started driving.

Sabrina had actually never been to this restaurant before. She walked through the glass doors, and she stopped at the hostess station.

She leaned to the left, then to the right, scanning through the different patrons. She figured that he would be alone.

"Table for two," she heard from behind her. Sabrina spun around, and she almost stumbled. She wasn't used to walking in high heels.

If she had fallen, then maybe this man would have grabbed her. He was familiar. In fact, they had already discussed earlier that day.

"Cale?" Sabrina asked.

"This time you remembered my name," he said, smiling. And yet, there was something about his tone of voice, something about his expression. He leaned in, violating her personal space without any hesitation. "Until I give you permission, you won't address me as anything but Sir or Master."

"A table for two," said the hostess. Apparently, she didn't hear any of his whispers.

Flushed, Sabrina didn't know what to do. Cale started to follow the hostess, only to pause a couple of feet later. He motioned for Sabrina to come with him.

She maneuvered between the tables, and then he reached out, taking her hand. His grip was strong, just like back at work.

Head spinning, Sabrina didn't know what was going on here. This man was an attorney, a guy who studied philosophy and probably sat around reading legal briefs.

And yet, he addressed her with the kind of forceful personality that Sabrina yearned to yield to. As he tugged her along, she wondered how it would feel to see this man naked, to strip for him, to bow down or to get down on her knees while he watched.

When she sat down, she pressed her lips together for a moment.

"What's going on here?"

"That's your second infraction," he told her, his tone unyielding.

All of a sudden, Sabrina felt as though she had been a bad girl who got sent to the principal's office. Even as she sat down, she realized something. She couldn't quite a look into his face.

"Second infraction?" Sabrina asked after another moment.

"Tonight, you were late. And just now, you failed to address me properly. If you want this meeting to continue, you had better behave yourself. You understand?"

She bristled. She thought she was getting angry, yet if it was only frustration or exasperation that surged through her body, then why did she feel that hint of arousal between her legs?

"Sabrina, I've been watching you for several weeks now. I think I have a good handle on who and what you are."

"Who am I...Sir?" She peeked up at him, and she saw the amusement playing around the corners of his eyes. Even if he wasn't smiling at her, he was certainly enjoying this.

"You are a very special kind of girl." He rested his elbows on the table, and he laced his fingers together. "Sabrina tell me if I'm wrong, but I believe you are a young woman who has worked really hard. You've probably dedicated yourself entirely to the service of others. You have focused only on what makes other people happy, because you've been told that pleasing others will somehow lead to your own satisfaction. But it hasn't, has it?"

She couldn't tell if it was the cadence of his voice or the simple confidence with which he spoke. In either case, she nodded her head. "Yes, Sir." There. She did it again. This time, she didn't hesitate.

She addressed him as Sir, almost like he deserved this extra dose of respect.

"Good," he told her. "I saw what you were reading."

Sabrina didn't know what to say this time. Instead, she swallowed.

He took that as his cue to continue. "Granted, that wasn't enough for me to decide to move all on its own. I've been watching you, like I said. You are an intriguing young woman, mostly because you are a paradox."

"How so...Sir?" Again, she appended his correct title at the last possible second.

Then again, if she truly irritated him, what was the worst that could happen? Intellectually, Sabrina told herself that she didn't need to worry about this man. Hell, in the strictest sense, she would probably be considered his boss. If she went to the investment bank and demanded a new consulting attorney, she was sure they would agree.

"Because you're powerful, but you want. You want to surrender. You want to give up."

"One could argue that lots of people in power have that fantasy."

"But this is a matter of degree," he said.

Sabrina wanted to ask more, but the server came around. Without even glancing up, Cale ordered for both of them. He got Sabrina the crab salad. For himself, he ordered steak. He also made sure that there would be both water and wine brought to their table. Again, he chose the vintage.

He spoke quickly and efficiently. The server made several notes, and then she scurried off. The girl who took their order didn't even bother trying to make any small talk. Perhaps she could sense that Cale would not be interested.

And because he took control, Sabrina didn't even register on the waitress's radar.

Once he was reasonably certain that the server was gone, Cale continued, "I understand that lots of women want to surrender in one way or another. Just consider the bodice ripper romances that seem to sell so well. Those are the girls who are secretly hoping that a billionaire will come by and scoop them out of their lives. But that's not you. You see, those women still want to have a great deal of control over their lives."

"I like control."

"No, you don't," he said, smirking. Maybe he didn't call that another infraction because he saw through the lie so easily. Or maybe she simply entertained him. "I can see it. Every time you have to go to another meeting, you want to pull out your fingernails. You're disgusted by the entire process."

"Okay, so they can get boring, but..."

"But nothing. You put on the collar and you played with it because you wanted to lose control. It's what you need, Sabrina."

She swallowed. Somehow, hearing this man use her name, here and now, it did something to her. It made her chest tighten. It made the heat gather between her legs. She had her hands under the table, and she squeezed her fingers together.

"How did you know I put it on?"

"The collar is network enabled. Whenever you put it on, I receive a notification."

Sabrina licked her lips, not sure what she should do with that information. Still looking downward, still feeling timid in the presence of this man, she asked another question, "May I ask, what are you proposing, Sir?" When those words left her lips, Sabrina glanced downward.

"Before you get that kind of information, you need to demonstrate that you deserve it. You need to show me that you can be a good girl."

She bristled, and she blushed. She didn't know what she was supposed to do, but she glanced up at him, and she sneered for just a moment. But then, he was already leaning forward a little bit more, and he dropped his voice for the sake of propriety. "Sabrina, stand up."

There. A command.

She didn't have to obey, yet if she defied it this man, she worried that this meeting, whatever it was, would come to an end. What if she disappointed him and he ordered her to leave?

Worse, what if he simply got up without a word and disappeared?

If he showed up at her office the next day, he could easily pretend that this meeting had never taken place. He could pretend that they were simply colleagues.

Nothing more.

That idea sent a stab of disappointment running through her gut. That's why she stood up.

"Now on, when I tell you to stand, your back needs to be straight, your hands need to be crossed at the small of your back, and your chest should be outstretched. Remember, when I tell you to stand, I'm putting you on display. In moments like this, you might as well be a doll or a puppet. Tell me you understand."

"I understand," she said, almost gritting her teeth. Anger, humiliation, and arousal swirled through her body like a storm front.

At this point, she couldn't exactly tell which of motion was going to win out.

"Assume the position."

She stood there, and she couldn't help herself. She glanced around the rest of the restaurant. Everyone in this place was powerful, simply because the prices were so high.

But she stood up, she lifted her chin, she straightened her back, and she crossed her wrists. Remaining seated, Cale swept his gaze up and down the length of her body. "You did a very nice job getting dressed, Sabrina."

"Thank you, Sir."

"Now go to the bathroom, take off your panties, and bring them back to me."

Her lips parted. This dress was already short enough. She didn't think she could risk walking around without her panties.

"What?"

"Right now."

Sabrina glanced back at him for just a moment. She thought she was going to complain or tell him that she couldn't possibly do something like that. And yet, as his eyes drilled back into her, Sabrina started moving. She turned around, and she walked toward the bathroom.

Before she made it five feet, he called out another command. He didn't raise his voice, and yet she had no problem hearing him anyway. "Oh, and Sabrina, let your hair down."

Although she didn't acknowledge either of his commands, Sabrina already found herself grabbing onto the hem of her skirt, pulling it down. She was decent, for the moment, yet she didn't know how much longer this would last.

She got to the ladies room, and locked the door without bothering to go into one of the stalls.

The bathroom was immaculate. She found herself standing on polished marble. In front of her, there was a huge mirror. She glanced back, and she still looked like a fierce, independent woman.

But then she reached up, and she pulled one of the bobby pins from her hair. Strands fell down along the right side of her body, cascading toward her bare shoulder. She repeated the process, and the rest of her mane fell down the nape of her neck.

Somehow, it felt like she was losing control.

That's precisely what happened. And then she made it even worse because she slipped her feet out of her pumps, and she reached down, pulling on the elastic of her panties. She took off her underwear, and she balled it up into her hand. Her panties were warm. Not only that, she realized that they were damp.

Whimpering, Sabrina glanced back at the mirror, and she saw the wild blush play along her cheeks. She didn't know if she could do this!

Shifting her weight from one foot to the other, she already knew that she could put her panties back on, and she could exit from the restaurant. She could retreat and never come back.

And yet, if she did that, she would never know exactly what Cale intended for her.

He was so strong, so handsome. She had never met a man like him. Sure, there were guys out there who thought that they could just take control, yet for them, that mostly meant acting like a jerk. When she saw this man, she saw something else, something new, someone who could control her without necessarily defaulting to cruelty.

And he was brilliant, it seemed.

Even if he hadn't developed the email attachment or the collar all on his own, he still found the resources to create both of them.

Bowing her head down, Sabrina surrendered to one simple fact.

She had no choice; she had to explore this.

She held her panties tight the palm of her hand, making sure that no one would see exactly what she was holding. Then she tugged down her skirt a little bit more, hoping that no one would be able to tell.

Obediently, she made her way back through the restaurant. She navigated between the tables, doing her best to scurry along as fast as she could on high heels. Her movements felt awkward, but she still did her best.

Without a word, Cale held out his hand. Palm up, he waited for her to deposit her panties. She gave them to him, and then she sat down. She was very careful to keep her knees together.

"Very nicely done," he said. "I think you're going to make an excellent slave girl."

"What, what does that mean, Sir?" Now that she no longer had on her panties, it was a lot easier for her to address him as her superior.

"It means you are going to belong to me, Sabrina. You put on the collar because you've been looking for someone to own you. You want someone to train you. So I'm going to do that. And you're going to be grateful."

She glanced downward. She stared at her thighs.

Just then, both their food and wine arrived. The server set down their plates, and as she did so, Cale took out his phone. He slid it across the white tablecloth.

"What is this?" Sabrina asked, looking down at the screen. His phone glowed with some sort of checklist.

"I do intend to own you," he told her. "However, there are going to be certain limits put in place. What I want you to decide, right now, is what you can handle."

Sabrina looked down at the list. She found sexual positions, types of punishment, and other forms of humiliation. She tightened her lips together once again as she stared at the screen.

"Eat."

Absentmindedly, she picked up her fork, and she stabbed into some lettuce. She brought it up to her mouth. She chewed, and she swallowed, all under his watchful gaze.

In some ways, Sabrina felt a little bit like a little girl. She couldn't help herself, not while she obeyed his command.

Hoping to distract herself, she looked down at the phone, and she scanned across the different options.

Each line came with three words: *Yes, No, Maybe.*

"Tell me what you can tolerate."

As she reviewed one line after another, Sabrina found her fingertips tingling. She started to poke the screen, making her decisions. She couldn't believe she was doing this. She couldn't believe she was doing this at a place like Donnely's.

Around her, the other patrons were probably discussing business. Sabrina was offering herself up for slavery.

More to the point, she knew exactly what this might entail because she had that collar in her purse. She had worn the metal ring around her neck, and she understood exactly what he could do to her.

It was designed for psychological control and manipulation. If he wanted to, he could actually condition her to forget her own name. He could train her to crawl or to yearn for the taste of his excitement.

"Sir, why should I trust you?"

"Because tonight, you're going to go home, and you're going to call up one of your minions. You're going to do a background check on me. That will assuage some of your concerns. After that, you're going to make a decision. You're going to decide whether or not you can trust me. I can promise you this, Sabrina. If you give yourself to me, you'll be my most valuable possession. I will train you, and I will turn you into anything and everything I want, but I can already see it in your eyes. You're going to enjoy it after you say yes."

As he spoke, Sabrina kept her eyes aimed down at his phone. She kept picking out different options, choosing between Yes, No, and Maybe.

For almost every line, she chose Yes.

When she got to the final decision, she indicated her answer, and he took his phone back. Sabrina glanced down at her meal, only to realize that she'd already eaten most of it.

"Of course, you're still going to have to earn this opportunity."

Sabrina almost squeaked. She maintained her composure, however.

"What, what do I have to do, Sir?"

"Spread your legs."

She swallowed, and yet she obeyed. With her knees hidden underneath the table, it wasn't like anyone else could tell exactly what she was doing anyway.

"Touch yourself."

"What? No, I can't!" she hissed back at him, practically snarling through her teeth. At the very least, she could be grateful that she didn't raise her voice enough for any of the other restaurant-goers to hear.

"Yes, you can. In fact, you will. But don't think I'm not adding that to your list of infractions, Sabrina."

She bristled at the implication, but then he tilted his head to the side. "Unless you want me to get up and leave right now, you're going to touch yourself. Take those cute little fingers of yours and slide them between your legs."

Sabrina glanced around the rest of the room. His voice cracked out, low but demanding, "No. Don't worry about them. Worry about me. I'm the one who's in charge here."

She turned her attention back to this man, and that's when she realized it. He could be her Master. He could own her. She just needed the courage to surrender.

In a way of its own accord, her hand drifted down between her legs. She parted her knees, and she touched herself, gliding her fingertips over her pussy. She was in the middle of a crowded restaurant, and conversation buzzed all around her.

Cale kept his gaze aimed right at her. "Good girl. Keep going."

She was getting wet and hot, so wet, so hot. She couldn't even name exactly why. She didn't know if it was the sensation of yielding to this man or if it had to be something else. In any case, Sabrina gave up.

Pretty soon, she was stroking her opening, down and up, down and up. Down and up.

"Stop."

"I can't," she whimpered, and her fingers kept going, dancing over her slit. She rubs downward, knowing full well that she could get caught any moment.

Just one or two more seconds, Sabrina kept touching herself until the pleasure cascaded through her skin. She felt them, these little and delicious ripples running all over her body.

When the orgasm faded away, she opened her eyes, and Cale was watching her, studying her. He had the tips of his fingers pressed together as he evaluated her.

"You're in a lot of trouble, young lady." He got up, and he walked over to her side of the table. He ran his fingers through her hair, he yanked her head back, and then he kissed her forehead.

Sabrina closed her eyes, thinking that he would press his lips down into her mouth.

He didn't.

By the time she opened her eyes, she saw that he was already walking back toward the exit.

That night, Sabrina went home. She went home, and she started masturbating. Driving back through the city proved to be surprisingly difficult. She kept squirming in her seat, thinking about what she could do.

More to the point, she wondered about Cale and what kind of decision he was going to make.

Because really, Sabrina already knew what her answer would be.

When she got home, she slammed the door shut, and she didn't even bother making it to her bedroom. No, she threw herself down onto her couch., She spread her legs, and she started stroking herself. She rubbed one hand against her breasts, alternating between her left and right nipple. The right was certainly more sensitive, but she loved this.

She relaxed into those sensations, and all the while, she thought of Cale. She thought of the man who might become something more...her Master.

It didn't seem possible.

She yearned to surrender, to yield herself up to someone strong and powerful, someone smart and dedicated. It could be him. He could be the one who would put her on the leash, who would use her and tease her and play with her, taking away every choice.

She swallowed, thinking about what he might do with her, what he might use her for.

In fact, she thought of those different items on his list.

She would never allow any of her boyfriends to have anal sex with her. But because he might be her Master, she said yes. Unequivocally. She thought about how it would feel, to be down on her stomach or positioned on her hands and knees.

She thought about what he might require her to wear. Maybe it would be a little harem slave outfit. Her wrists could be manacled. Or maybe he would require her to go to work with a vibrator wedged between her legs. It would be remote-controlled, and he would hold the device.

During any one of those boring meetings, he could surreptitiously press a button, and she would be tormented with the potential for ecstasy.

Sabrina rubbed and stroked herself. She caressed herself, teasing those different parts of her body until she arched her back, her lips quivered, and she gasped through the pleasure. Hot ecstasy ran through her body, taking away all doubts, all worries, all concerns.

And a few minutes later, after just a little bit of rest, she did it all over again.

Chapter 6

When she woke up, Sabrina didn't know how to articulate exactly what she was feeling. It seemed like a mixture of energized excitement and worn-out exhaustion. How many times did she touch herself last night? How many orgasms did she experience, first on her couch, and then in her bedroom?

In those first couple of seconds, she thought about calling in sick.

But then she rolled over, and she forced herself to shower. The hot water along her naked skin certainly helped. This time, Sabrina resisted the temptation to start touching herself again.

Even if she didn't pet her clit, Sabrina still felt that rush of excitement flowing through her body.

She got dressed. Today, she put on a simple, pencil skirt with a lavender blouse. After that, she dried her hair, and she went in to work.

"Do I have any meetings today?" Sabrina asked Kyle when she came up to her office.

"Uh, yes," he answered. "One of the lawyers, Larsen, asked for a private meeting with you."

Sabrina opened her mouth, and she couldn't think of something to say.

"Is everything all right?" Kyle asked her.

She coughed; she cleared her throat. "Yes, everything is fine. Um, what time is the meeting?"

"In about ten minutes," he replied.

"Okay, good. Great. Excellent," she said, stammering like she was some nervous school girl. Her assistant looked back at her like he wanted to ask if something was wrong, but he thought better of it, and Sabrina was already retreating back into her office. She closed the door, and she went over to the desk. She fell into her seat.

Normally, she would have the same routine. She would have gotten herself some coffee and checked through her emails. Today, she ran her teeth along her bottom lip.

That's when her phone buzzed. She nearly jumped when she heard that sound. But then, she grabbed it, and she saw she had a text message. It was from an unknown number, and then she saw the message, and her jaw dropped open.

Take off your panties. Be ready to present them to me when I arrive.

Sabrina immediately got up. She stared down at her phone, almost like she thought it was some dangerous creature that might jump up and attack her at any moment. She started pacing, walking back and forth.

Even as she moved, she could feel the arousal and heat gather right between her inner thighs. She was getting damp again, and she actually crossed her knees for a moment. She kept thinking about what she should do or say.

Finally, she exhaled through her teeth, and she took off her panties.

A moment later, someone knocked on her door.

"Come in," she called out, grateful that her voice didn't break or crack.

The door opened, and Cale walked in. "Good morning," he said, loud enough for her assistant to hear. Then he closed the door. "You owe me a decision."

Sabrina stared down at the floor. She didn't know if she could do this. With every second, she wondered if cowardice would take hold of her tongue.

But then, she spoke. "Yes."

"Another infraction," he told her.

She glanced up, confused. But he was holding out his hand, so she crossed of the distance between them, and she gave him her panties.

Cale cut the distance between them. He pressed his chest up against hers, and she tried to retreat back, but his hand already shot out, taking a firm grip at the back of her neck. He didn't hurt her, yet he made it abundantly clear that she wasn't going to be able to rush off, not until he released her.

"Sabrina, if you want to be my bimbo slave, you're going to have to get down on your knees and beg for the privilege."

"Beg?" This time, her voice squeaked. She didn't sound dignified or powerful. She certainly didn't come off as any kind of executive.

"That's right. If you want to be my slave, you're going to beg for the privilege. And then, if you do a very, very good job, I will accept you as my pet and plaything."

Sabrina wanted to tell him that she didn't know if she could do this, and yet she fell down onto her knees. This was her office, and it was supposed to be her position of power. Yet she kept her eyes aimed down at his black, leather shoes. "Please, Sir, may I be your bimbo?"

"So you want to be dumb? You want to be a silly girl who just giggles and thinks about sex and pleasing her Master all the time? Is that what you want?"

She was so close to him. In fact, because she was on her knees, she had no problem seeing the outline of his erection. Realizing that he was hard only made her even hotter.

"Yes, please. Please, can you train me to be a dumb girl? Will you train me to be your obedient bimbo? I want to serve you, Sir. I want you to be my Master. Please, I promise I'll be good for you. I promise I'll be obedient."

"I think obedience is going to be a challenge for a girl like you," he said. "After all, you already have so many infractions against you."

"Yes, Sir." She risked a glance up at this man.

"There's something you need to understand, Sabrina. If you agree to be my slave, this isn't going to be a game. I'm going to train you. I'm going to teach you to be completely obedient. You understand?"

"Yes, I understand," she replied. He explained all of it last night. He would take care of her. He would own her, he would control her, and he would ensure that she always had a place at his feet.

She thought about what she was offering up.

Everything, really.

"Kiss my feet."

This time, she didn't have as much trouble. She bent down, and she pressed her lips into his shoes. She could smell the aroma of leather, and it sent another thrill running down her back.

At the same time, she thought about what she would do or say if people happened to walk in at this moment. She didn't remember locking the door. Kyle could burst inherent any moment, and she would be on her knees, kissing another man's shoes.

"Look up at me."

She obeyed.

"Fetch your collar."

Sabrina immediately scurried back over to her purse. She reached in, and she had no trouble finding the device. When she turned back around, she saw Cale already had his phone out. His thumb danced along the screen, and putting in one command or another.

"Kneel in front of me. Give me the collar."

She obeyed both orders, and he took the metal ring.

"Are you ready to begin your training?"

She inhaled, and she held her breath for a couple of seconds. This was it. She looked back at the silver device, studying the contours of the way the light played along the curves. If he put that around her, then he would really be in control. He would be able to alter the basic foundations of her psychology.

Her breathing turned quick, her heart was pounding, and she said just one word.

"Yes."

He slipped the collar around her neck, and then he entered the command. He confirmed the parameters, and the lock engaged.

She remained there, down on the floor. Most of her weight was braced and her knees, but she was bent forward slightly, her palms pressed down as well.

"Sabrina, you are now my bimbo. Sometimes, I'm going to allow you to pretend to be an independent woman who gets to make her own decisions. But most of the time, you're going to be just like this."

"Yes, Sir."

"Now, you have a full six infractions against you."

"Six?"

"Make that seven," he replied.

Sabrina glanced up at him, her eyes big and nervous. She didn't remember messing up seven different times! She was about to tell him that this wasn't fair, only then she noticed the smirk curling along his lips.

That's when she understood. This was a test.

"Yes, Master," she said.

"Seven shocks," he said. He held up his phone, and he tapped the screen.

The first jolt launched through her body, making her twitch. The second blast of electricity hit her just a few seconds later. Her eyes started to water. The third and fourth strikes flashed through her skin, and she began to whimper. She couldn't believe that this was happening.

It hurt way more than she expected. She fell down onto her side.

The fifth and sixth blasted into her, and she couldn't breathe. She couldn't think.

Cale straddled her. He rolled her down onto her back, and he looked into her eyes. "Don't make a sound," he commanded.

She pressed her lips together, but then the seventh and final rush lit up the pain receptors all over her body. Her lips parted, but she somehow managed to keep herself silent.

"Good girl. Now, we can start fresh. Strip for me."

Sabrina reached up, and she almost touched the collar. Then she remembered that if her fingertips made contact, it would deliver another blow. She stopped herself, and she looked back at this man.

"Master, may I make a request?"

"You may."

"Would you lock the door, please?"

"Why would I do that?"

She blushed brightly. Then again, she couldn't tell if the heat playing along her skin had more to do with the barrage of electrical punishments she had already endured. "Please, Master. Can you lock the door?"

"Are you worried people would realize what you are now?"

"Yes!"

"But I already know how that makes you feel. You want people to know that you're just a silly girl. You don't want them to respect you anymore. Don't worry. We're going to take care of that."

She narrowed her eyes at him.

"Go sit up on your desk and touch yourself."

Sabrina didn't start moving right away. That's why he tapped the screen, and another jolt of electricity shot through her body, catching her off guard. She let out a little yelp, and then she froze, waiting, wondering if her assistant was going to pop his head in to ask what was going on.

She got lucky.

Maybe Kyle was off getting a cup of coffee, or maybe he had his ear buds in. Either way, Sabrina didn't have to explain herself.

But she did need to move. She got up on her hands and knees. She lifted herself back up onto her feet, and she started walking. She went back to her desk, and she sat there on the edge, exactly as he had commanded.

"Good girl. Stay right there. I'll be back in a few minutes."

He walked out of the door, and he closed it again. Sabrina kept listening, hoping that she would hear the telltale sound of the lock engaging. She didn't. She was still vulnerable, seated there on her desk with her legs spread.

That's when she heard something, this clicking sound. She looked around, and then she realized that it was coming from the collar around her neck. Instinctively, she reached up to touch it, only to stop herself at the last moment again.

What was it doing?

Sabrina decided that she wanted to check it out. Besides, she probably had some time, so she slipped off of the desk, and she was going to go back to one of the drawers. She thought she had a makeup mirror.

Electricity buzzed through her skin.

Cale wasn't even in the room!

Then she remembered the built in MRI, how it could detect certain physiological and autonomic responses.

The collar determined that she was moving, so it punished her.

Her eyes watered again, her lower lip trembled, and Sabrina scurried back into position. She seated herself on the edge of the desk, and she got another dose of electricity anyway! It wasn't fair! She looked around, and she was about to start asking what was wrong, even though she was alone in the room. Then she remembered her knees. She spread her legs.

Bracing herself, she wondered if there's going to be another jolt.

From one second into the next, she waited.

Nothing happened.

After a few more seconds, she let out a sigh of relief, grateful that she didn't get punished again.

Eventually, the door opened, and Sabrina called out for Cale to come in, even though he had already stepped across the threshold.

"Don't worry. Your assistant isn't out there right now."

"I'm glad," she said.

"Are you? Are you really?" He was mocking her, but Sabrina just kept her lips closed.

"It's okay. I can see it in your eyes. You're probably more aroused right now than you ever have been before. Is that right?"

"No," she told him. She braced herself, wondering if there's going to be another shock of electricity.

Nothing happened. She just lied to her Master, but she wasn't punished for it.

Or so she thought.

"Oh, okay. Since you're not aroused at all, then you don't mind if I do this," he said, pulling something from his pocket. She saw that it was a lavender dildo. In fact, the color perfectly matched her blouse.

He took that implement, and he touched it, first to her shin, then to her knees, then to her inner thigh. He stroked it along her flesh slowly, tauntingly. Every second sent fresh tingles running through her body, especially because Sabrina knew that she couldn't move. If she deviated from her current position, the collar would deliver another painful shock.

So she stayed there, doing her best to pretend that this didn't affect her.

"Admit the truth. Tell me you're a horny little slut who wants an orgasm."

"No. I can't," she said in a small voice.

"It's okay. I expected this to happen. I know that you're going to test the limits of your newfound slavery, Sabrina. You're going to push the boundaries as much as you can. But there are always going to be consequences. That's what you need to understand." He pressed to the tip of the dildo up against her pussy. He stroked her once, then twice. Her body was so ready for that kind of teasing.

When he pushed the dildo forward, penetrating her, she could only inhale and exhale to deal with those sensations. The pleasure built up in her body, but she wanted more. She needed more.

Closing her eyes, she did her best maintain a façade of detached and neutrality. She was close, so incredibly close.

Then she heard the sounds of the collar clicking again.

"What, what does this do, Master?" When she asked, she sounded frantic.

When she looked up at him, she saw him smirking back at her.

"It's you aren't aroused, you won't mind if I put you on a regimen of orgasm denial."

"What?" Sabrina squeaked.

He reached out, and he patted her on the head. "I have to go take care of some work. You probably have some business you need to deal with as well. Have fun." He pinched her cheek, he turned around, and he walked right out the door.

Sabrina watched him go, her brows crinkled with confusion. This didn't make any sense.

Orgasm denial? What was he talking about?

Once he closed the door behind him, Sabrina slid off of the desk, and she looked around the rest of her office. Okay, so maybe he was right. Maybe she needed to focus on her work.

First, she looked around for her panties, hoping that maybe he had dropped them. No, he took them with him. Her skirt was longer than what she had on last night, but she still felt vulnerable.

"I can do this," she said.

Sabrina went back to her desk, and she back down. The moment she swallowed, she felt the metal ring around her neck. She wasn't going to be able to get this off, she couldn't even touch it.

Quickly, she logged into her computer, and she checked her calendar. Fortunately, she didn't have any meetings today, but that didn't mean people weren't going to stop by. There would probably be questions. She was the leader of this enterprise, after all.

She didn't like being a wimp, but Sabrina got up, and she crept over to the door. She opened it just a crack, and she peeked out. She saw Kyle, sitting at his desk.

"Kyle, I'm really busy today. Make sure no one disturbs me right now. Okay?"

"Sure thing," he said. Before her assistant could say anything else, she closed the door. This time, she was doubly certain to lock it.

Once she had the relative protection of her door, Sabrina walked back to her desk, and with every step, she could feel that desire build back inside of her.

She already knew that she wasn't supposed to touch herself, but she sat down, and she decided to experiment.

Sabrina reached up, and she cupped both of her breasts. She touched her thumbs to the fabric just above her nipples. With every second, she braced herself, thinking that she might get an electrical shock.

Nothing happened. She touched herself more and more, and then she stopped, still waiting for that inevitable dose of punishment.

It never came.

Maybe the collar didn't work as well as he thought. Or maybe Cale just figured that he could tease her into submission.

That's when she decided to spread her legs and touch herself some more. She didn't even have to worry about her panties. She slipped one hand under her skirt, and she stroked her crevice. She lightly grazed the pad of her fingertips along her opening. She shivered, and she waited, thinking that there might be another smack of painful energy.

Nothing.

A triumphant smirk ran along her lips. She started to touch herself, working her fingers between her legs. Every time she inhaled, she could still feel that stiff resistance of metal around her neck. She didn't know exactly what her Master had attempted, but if she could sneak in an orgasm or five, then she'd do it!

She felt like such a naughty little girl. That disobedience only fueled her desires, making it impossible for her to resist. She was close, so close!

The collar came to life, delivering a painful jolt. It knocked her deep into her chair, and her hand flew away from her pussy. She stopped, and she could only breathe, her eyes wet.

Quivering, almost hyperventilating, Sabrina reached up for the collar. This time, she really did forget about the countermeasure, so it punished her again. Another jolt jumped through her skin, lighting up pain receptors all over her body. That's when her hands fell back down into her lap.

Her phone buzzed, and she grabbed it, already knowing that it was going to be a message from her Master.

Don't be a bad bimbo.

He knew!

Obviously, he has some sort of connection between his phone and the device around her neck. So it made sense that he would be able to monitor her behaviors.

It almost felt like he was watching her.

And yet, that just turned her on even more. The painful burst of energy certainly disrupted her orgasm. She didn't get off, but the rest of her body didn't just calm down automatically. No, the fact that she wasn't going to be allowed to reach that point of completion only made it worse. Sabrina pressed her lips together, and she tried to think about what she was going to do.

She wanted to find some way to get off, yet that was already becoming an impossibility.

Gritting her teeth, she quickly came to one conclusion. She didn't have any choice. She had to simply focus on her work.

So she sat down at her desk, and she did her best to concentrate.

It was tough, really tough.

First, she opened up her email, but none of these messages seemed all that important. They couldn't excite her.

After just a few minutes, she closed out her browser, and she tried to think of something else she should do.

Nothing came to mind.

She couldn't stand this.

Sabrina got up, and she went back to the door. Pressing her ear to the wood, she waited. After a few seconds, she could pick out the sounds of clicking and typing. Kyle was probably right there. She couldn't just sneak out of her office. Besides, everyone in the building knew her name. If she walked around in a collar, everyone would know.

Sabrina walked back across the room, and she picked up her phone. She wanted to send a text to her Master, to beg him to come back. Maybe he would reconsider?

Then she realized something. Although she received text messages from him, they always came from an unknown number. She couldn't just hit reply.

Tapping her fingers against her desktop, she needed to calm down. But just the fact that she wasn't allowed to touch herself, to climax, was enough to make her desperately wet. With every second, she wanted to move. It felt like she might start crawling out of her own skin!

This wasn't fair. She couldn't do this!

That's when she remembered something. She slammed the bottom drawer of her desk open. It rolled and clicked. She looked down, and she snatched an old sweater. It was a turtleneck!

Grinning, she finally felt like something was going her way.

Sabrina pulled it on, and then she bowed her head down as she retreated out of her office. She walked as fast as she could back to the stairwell. She skipped the elevator, worrying that there might be some of her employees in there.

She went down one floor, and then she searched through some of the offices. That's when she saw it, one placard.

Cale Larsen.

He had some office space assigned to him because he spent so much time here. She went to the door, and she knocked, tapping her knuckles. "Hello?"

No response.

She glanced up and down the hallway. Fortunately she was alone.

"Master? Are you there?"

"Come in, slave," she heard.

She put her fingers to the handle, and she stepped across the threshold. There he was, seated at his desk. Since this was basically borrowed workspace, he hadn't bothered to decorate.

"It's good to see you, slave. You didn't hold out very long, I see. Did you get very much work done?"

Sabrina shook her head. She was blushing brightly, realizing how pathetic and foolish she must have looked. Seriously, he turned off her ability to have an orgasm for just a few minutes, and then she went scurrying through the office, desperate to find the one man who could get her off?

"Master, I was hoping that maybe you would turn off the collar?"

"I might, but you'll have to earn the privilege of an orgasm."

"Earn it? How?"

"I have some work I need to do, but it would be nice if I had your pretty mouth under the desk."

Right away, she understood exactly what he meant. He wanted her to suck him off while he conducted business.

The idea aroused and embarrassed her like nothing else. She could feel the shame and desire pounded through her skin.

In fact, her hand actually hovered right above her crotch. She really, really wanted to slide her fingers over her clit. She wanted to touch herself until that rush of ecstasy exploded along every inch of her skin. She wanted it so badly!

"Get down on your hands and knees and crawl."

Sabrina bristled, but she also obeyed. Even as she gritted her teeth, she made her way across the floor. He had already rolled his seat back, so there was plenty of room for her.

Just before she ducked under the desk, he changed his mind. At least a little bit. "Oh, and get naked."

"What?"

"You heard me bimbo. You're just a little slut who wants to be taken. You want sex. You're a horny girl, so you're going to do as you're told. Get naked."

She did her best not to react, but her entire body tensed. She couldn't help herself. It was an automatic reaction. Sabrina made a fist. She forced herself to relax, and then she got up on her knees. While this man watched, she peeled off her sweater. From there, she unbuttoned her blouse, and she took off her bra.

She didn't make eye contact with him. She couldn't.

The shame kept pounding into her skin, every moment another reminder that she was giving up everything to this man. And what if someone walked in here? What if someone saw her?

She didn't know what she would do. There'd be no way to reclaim her reputation.

She discarded every article of clothing. When she took off her skirt, she no longer had anything on, nothing except the collar, that is.

"Very nice," he said. "Proceed."

She crawled under his desk, and she positioned herself, just waiting. He rolled back, and she placed her chin between his legs. He unzipped his pants, and he took out his shaft. There was his cock, big and hard. The tip was already damp with his excitement.

"Have you ever gone down on a guy before?"

"Yes, Master."

"Have you ever done it like this?"

"No, Master."

"You need to be good for me and ask permission. Tell me you're looking forward to sucking my cock while I deal with a conference call."

Her cheeks got really warm. In fact, it felt like every inch above her skin rose several degrees. Even the tips of her ears heated up.

And yet, Sabrina really wanted her orgasm. She needed that pleasure, so she yielded to this man. "Please, Master. I'm really looking forward to sucking your cock. May I?" She giggled like a silly girl, but then he reached down, and he put his hand on the back of her head. He didn't say anything to her. Instead, he nudged her forward, and she opened her mouth. She licked him once, and then she tightened her lips around his shaft. She got him slick with her saliva. She moved her head down and up, down and up, down and up.

In the meantime, she could hear his phone. He had the speaker on.

She sucked and licked while he talked to several other people. They sounded important.

At first, she tried to focus. She almost wondered if this was going to be important, like it was something she needed to hear.

But then she reminded herself of one simple fact. She was just a bimbo. She was just a silly girl! If her Master wanted to talk about business, then it wasn't her place to question his decision. It wasn't her place to think at all.

She started to giggle again, and he rolled back just a little bit so that he could look down into her eyes.

"You're a good little slut," he told her. That's when he grabbed onto her hair and he started to move her head faster. He jerked her down and up, down and up.

"Get ready to swallow," he told her.

That's when she started whimpering. No! She couldn't swallow! She had never done that.

And yet, he wasn't about to release her.

He kept going, working her face against his cock until he was ready. He closed his eyes, he held his breath, and then he enjoyed the sensations of his shaft pulsating. He enjoyed his orgasm. He savored every moment of it even as he splashed his load against the back of her throat.

Sabrina didn't have any other choice. She started swallowing.

She drank down his come, swallowing through one gulp after another.

Of course, she hated doing this. Of course, she wanted to retreat back, yet there was nowhere else for her to go. She had already been sucking his cock for several minutes, perhaps as long as half an hour.

And when he finished with her, he put his hand on her forehead, and he nudged her back, but he didn't roll his chair away, to let her out.

Apparently, Sabrina would remain on her hands and knees, under his desk.

She positioned herself at the back, resting her head against the frame of the desk. She sat there, and she waited like a good little bimbo, wondering when her Master would be done.

Eventually, he turned off his phone, and he rolled back. He looked down at his naked little bimbo.

"Do you want an orgasm?"

"Yes, please Master!"

"Good," he said. He rolled back a little bit farther. "Come up here and sit on my leg."

"What, what you going to do with me?"

"Simple. If you want your orgasm, you're going to get it, but you aren't going to be allowed to use your hands."

"I, I don't understand." She moved out from under the desk, but this still didn't make sense to her.

"Get up here and ride my leg."

Her eyes widened to the size of quarters. No! No way! She couldn't do something, something like that!"

"Please, Master, can I do something..."

Before she had the chance to finish, he grabbed his phone, and he pressed another button. Electricity shot through her body, robbing her of the air she needed to speak. Bowing her head down, she realized that her Master wasn't making requests. He was giving her an order, so she had better obey.

She got up, and she positioned herself right there on his thigh. She held her hands behind her back, and she pressed forward, touching her breasts into his chest. "That's right. There you go. You're doing a good job," he said to her.

She grimaced. She hated this, but there was nothing else she could do.

Lowering herself down, she rubbed herself against his leg. Closing her eyes, she gripped her wrists tightly with her hands. She wasn't cuffed or restrained, yet she felt ultimately trapped. There is no way she could get out of this, and she knew it.

"Good," her Master said to her. "Very good."

Biting into her lower lip, she started to press her body into his. It felt good, really good. More importantly, she had her Master's permission. She could do this, and he wouldn't punish her.

In fact, he would only discipline her if she tried to stop. So she kept going, pushing her body into his, rubbing her body against his. It felt right. Even though the humiliation and shame didn't go away, she kept going, rubbing herself up against this man like some wanton slut.

"Do you know what I love most about this?"

"What, Master?"

"You look just like a little dog. A dog humping my leg. I guess that makes you my bitch now, doesn't it?"

She rubbed herself a little bit harder, a little bit faster.

"Answer me."

"Yes, Master. Yes, I'm your bitch, Master!"

As that final syllable left her lips, Sabrina came. She panted, and she moaned, savoring the ecstasy until she actually fell off of his lap. She landed down on her hands and knees.

"Well done. Now go fetch me something to eat."

Her Master was generous. He allowed her to put on her skirt and her blouse, her shoes and even the turtleneck sweater. Even so, she ducked out of his office, and she looked around, terrified that someone might be there. Even if she looked reasonably put together, she worried about her aroma. She still had the taste of his come on her tongue.

Altogether, she probably smelled like sex.

He gave her a command, however, so she had to obey. She took the elevator down, and she was very grateful she had the car to herself. From there, she walked to the deli across the street.

She purchased him a sandwich and some chips. She got him a soda, and she carried it all back up.

This time, luck wasn't on her side.

"I haven't seen you around much today," said one of her colleagues. "Is everything okay?"

"I'm fine," she replied, keeping her head down.

Fortunately for her, the doors dinged open, and she rushed back out into the hallway. Sabrina didn't even glance over her shoulder, and she was grateful she didn't hear a question about how this wasn't even her floor.

When she got back to his door, she knocked once, and she waited.

Again, she glanced in both directions before asking to enter. "Master, may I come in?"

"Enter," he said to her.

Sabrina brought him his lunch, and then she stood there, feeling awkward, like she didn't know what she was supposed to do.

"Kneel," he said, pointing down to the floor. Like a good bimbo, she obeyed without question.

While she watched, he unwrapped his sandwich. He popped open the bag of chips, and he poured some of them out.

"Sabrina, have you eaten yet?" asked her Master.

"No, Sir."

"Okay," he told her, and he ripped off a piece of the sandwich. He placed it gingerly in the palm of his hand, and he held it out for her.

Sabrina reached out with her fingertips, and she was about to pick it up, but he clicked his tongue. "No, no," he told her. "Right now, I'm feeding you. So how should you eat?"

"...You want me to eat out of the palm of your hand..." It wasn't a question.

"That's right," he said to her.

Sabrina hesitated. She looked around, almost like she hoped for some other solution. Only then, he grabbed his phone. He already had the punishment application available on the screen.

"No, Sir! You don't need to..."

Sabrina didn't get the opportunity to finish her sentence. He tapped the button, and the collar delivered another sharp strike of electricity. The energy flashed through her body, making her nerves tense with pain.

She stumbled down, only to land on her knuckles. Then she sat up again, and there he was, still holding out the food in the palm of his hand.

"Thank you, Sir."

Sabrina leaned in, and she ate out of his hand.

"Good girl."

Some mustard spilled onto his skin. "Lick it up," he commanded.

"Yes, Sir." She obeyed, lapping his palm with the flat of her tongue.

Smiling at her, he watched.

To think, this young woman had been so strong and so powerful and so independent only a few days before. Now he had her, and utterly helpless.

"Very nicely done. Now some more," he ordered. He took another piece, and he held it out for her.

This time, Sabrina didn't hesitate, nor did she question his decision. If he decided that she had to eat out of his hand, then she needed to do it. There wasn't any question, and she couldn't debate it.

For several more minutes, he ate some of his sandwich, and he fed her. He enjoyed some chips, and the Sabrina kept hoping that he might forget about her.

Except for one thing.

Even though she tried to ignore it, there was still that yearning deep within her body. She had one orgasm. That was true. But it wasn't enough. Her body yearned for more. She felt like an addict, and the only one who could satiate her happened to be sitting in the chair next to her.

As he finished his sandwich, Sabrina looked down at the floor. "Master?"

"What is it, bimbo?"

She bristled at the title. Even if she had fantasized about this before, she still couldn't bat away that casual insult. After all, Sabrina had been one of the intellectual girls back in high school and college. Well-read and focused on her studies, she always derided the other girls, the ones who focused on putting on the right makeup or picking out the best dress.

"Would you like to have sex with me, Master?"

There. The question was out on the air.

He turned away from his desk, and he looked down at her. In those first couple of heartbeats, Sabrina couldn't meet his gaze. She tried to look away, only he touched two fingers to the underside of her chin. He forced her to look back up at him.

"Do you want me to bend you over my desk so that I can fuck you?"

Swallowing, Sabrina had no choice but to tell this man the truth. "Yes, please."

"You're still horny, aren't you?"

"Yes, Master. Very."

"Stand."

Sabrina got back up onto her feet. It felt good.

"Tell me that you're going to do whatever I want. Giggle and beam just like a bimbo. I want to look into your eyes and see that you are utterly devoid of any real intelligence."

"Yes, Master. I'll try," she promised. Then she dipped her head down, and she looked to the floor. Concentrating, she did her best to clear the intellect from her head. For such a long time, she had worried about being sharp and competitive. Whether she had to fight with other students or other business people, Sabrina had always been determined to win.

This time, she didn't have a competitor.

Instead, she held onto one goal, one desire: please this man.

"Like, I really want to have sex with you, Sir! Please, please can we have sex? I'd love for you to bend me over that desk!" As she spoke, she wobbled her head from side to side. Her voice rose, taking on the high pitch of an excited cheerleader. "Please, Master! Like, I want to be a good girl for you! I want to be used and stuff!" She giggled some more, and then she followed her instincts. She reached up, and she twirled one finger through her hair.

Without a word, Cale stood, and he grabbed her by the back of her neck. He pushed her forward, bending her over the desk, and then he smacked her ass.

"Like, what was that for?" squealed the bimbo.

"Nothing," he told her. "I just really wanted to spank you."

Sabrina pressed her lips together, but then she remembered her place. "Thank you, Master. Would you like to spank me again? It felt really good."

That was only half wrong. After all, once that hand flashed down and when she felt that sting along the curve of her ass, Sabrina did experience something, a rush of arousal.

She couldn't explain it. None of her boyfriends had ever spanked her. She never thought about it all. And yet, when his hand came down and when she heard that clap, she experienced a hot rush of yearning.

"Only because you asked so nicely," he told her. A Sabrina tried to brace herself. It didn't do any good.

His hand flew down several more times, striking into her unprotected rear. At first, Sabrina didn't think it mattered. Yes, it stung, but those sensations drilled into her. She could feel them flashing through her body, like one burst of lightning after another. Yes, they disappeared, yet the lingering sensations drove her wild.

Sabrina didn't understand it, yet her body became desperate. She could feel it, that throbbing between her legs. She whimpered, and her eyes watered. A couple of tears ran down her cheeks, and she panted, gasping.

When she tried to speak, she couldn't even tell if she wanted him to stop or to continue.

And then, he lowered the zipper on his pants, he took out his cock, and he leaned inward. He teased her with the tip of his cock for just a second or two before he pushed himself forward, sliding his member deep into her opening. He buried his cock all the way to the hilt, and he held onto her hips.

"Maybe you need a little bit more," he decided.

This time, she started shaking her head. Sabrina distinctly tried to tell him to stop, yet he was her Master. He could do whatever he wanted with her little body.

More to the point, she loved it. When she felt his hand on her skin, she shivered with anticipation. But he spanked her, it turned her on. And when he pulled back gently, almost withdrawing altogether, her entire body shook.

Sabrina needed this and so much more.

"What are you?"

"I'm your bimbo slave, Master!" This time she didn't talk like an airhead. Instead, she just cried out those words, panting like some desperate slut.

He pushed forward and pulled back, taking what he wanted from this girl. He claimed her. Sure, she had swallowed his come but this invasion made it clear that she couldn't try to resist. She couldn't argue or fight. She belonged to him.

He worked her harder and faster.

"Come for me," he commanded, squeezing her ass. His fingertips pressed down into her cute little rump. Pain and pleasure mixed together, swirling into this unstoppable storm deep within her frame.

The movements of his hips, the singing of her nerves, and of the undeniable passion made it impossible for Sabrina to stop the orgasm.

"Come for me, you little slut!" He spanked her again. Just as the pain sizzled through her skin, Sabrina climaxed. She panted, gasping like she couldn't possibly take in enough air.

That's when he grabbed onto her hair and pulled. Another wave of pain washed over her, but it was good. It was so, so good. Sabrina stops thinking. She stopped worrying. She surrendered entirely to what her body could give her.

And that's when she felt it, the way his cock throbbed. He blew his load, working her harder, faster, deeper.

Her pussy clenched around him, squeezing out every drop of his excitement. And when he finished, he was still hard.

"Get on your knees so he can lick me clean."

Sabrina turned around. Her legs wobbled, and she could barely stand straight, but that didn't matter. Her Master had given her a command, so she needed to obey. She needed to please this man.

She positioned herself before her Master, and she got back down onto her knees. He got up, and he looked down at her. He ran his fingers over the top of her head. He gripped her hair, and he forced her mouth back. That's when he pushed forward with his shaft, touching the tip of his erection to her mouth.

First, she started by licking him. She slid the flat of her tongue over his contours. But apparently, that wasn't enough for her Master. He took a hold of her hair once again, and he pulled her face closer. At the same time, he moved his hips toward her lips, forcing her to take one-inch after another.

"Suck me clean, slut."

Slut. Bimbo.

Those words cut down into her psyche, reminding Sabrina of her newfound position, her newfound status. She licked and sucked. She moved her head forward and back.

It wasn't enough to satisfy her Master. Still holding onto her hair, he forced her head forward and back, faster and faster. He wasn't done with this girl. He wasn't going to let her stop just yet.

Finally, he released her.

Sabrina stumbled back, and he leaned forward. He rested his elbows on the edges of his knees. "Be a good girl and go back to work. I have another assignment for you later."

"Yes, Master."

As Sabrina made her way back to her office, she kept looking down at herself. Once again, she used the stairwell. Her feet boomed against each step as she pulled herself up.

Truthfully, she felt exhausted. As she made her way back down the corridor to her office, she didn't even check to see if anyone else was around. Fortunately, Kyle was not at his desk. As his boss, she might have wondered where he got off to.

Not today.

She opened up her door, and she walked through. She closed it and locked it and stumbled over to her desk. She collapsed back down, and then she reached up, touching her turtleneck. She didn't actually touch the collar, so it didn't activate. It didn't punish her.

She had a metal ring around her neck, a reminder of her position.

"I'm a bimbo slave," she said, wondering precisely what this would mean.

r a while, Sabrina decided that she couldn't just stay ...r office. Yes, she had eaten a little bit of Cale's sandwich, but it wasn't enough. Eventually, she opened the door just a crack, and she found Kyle typing away at his keyboard.

"Can you go get me some lunch?"

"Sure, what would you like?"

"I already emailed you my request," she said. She closed the door again, and she was very careful to lock it.

Despite her exhaustion, Sabrina was at a point of getting some work done. She needed to feel the normalcy of typing on her keyboard, of clicking on messages, of accomplishing something.

Kyle came back, and he knocked gently on the door. She opened it for him, and she grabbed her sandwich. It felt good to get back to her desk. She chomped away through the bread, meat, and cheese.

But once she finished and the hunger had abated, Sabrina didn't know exactly what to do. She glanced back at her computer, and she wondered.

She wondered what she wanted.

She wondered what she should do.

She wondered who she was becoming.

Running her teeth along her bottom lip, Sabrina thought about her Master once again. She considered how she felt about him, what he inspired within her. Theoretically, they had known one another for several weeks, but she only started paying attention to him when he sent her that attachment.

Sabrina still didn't understand exactly how he was able to devise something like that. Eventually, she could only come to one conclusion. He was brilliant. Whether he developed the technology himself or he found someone else who could do it, it really didn't matter.

And she swallowed again, feeling the solid metal around her neck.

With her stomach full, Sabrina decided that she needed to stop thinking. She needed to stop worrying about her work. Because really, she couldn't explain why it mattered. She ran a website dedicated to one principle: profit. She didn't make the world a better place. She didn't improve any lives.

Seated at her desk, she stared out into space. She seemed so vacant, so innocent. This young woman just didn't convey any sense of focus. She seemed to float, thinking about everything that transpired over the last few hours.

Again and again, she thought of how this was her building. Sure, she didn't own it, but it was in her company's name, her company's logo out on the front. She sat through those meetings to get everything in place.

And now?

Now this brown haired girl had lost her panties. She lost her underwear, yet she did get something else.

The collar.

For a long time, Sabrina didn't think or move. She felt a little bit like a doll, discarded and left behind until her Master decided to come back for her. She didn't know how long she'd have to wait. Yet this time, she didn't get impatient or frustrated.

Sitting there at her desk almost seemed like floating. Easy and simple, she surrendered to the fatigue. Without slumping down, Sabrina collected her thoughts until the phone buzzed again.

Tentative, she reached out, brushing her fingertips along the plastic exterior. Sabrina couldn't remember setting her cell down, but it vibrated against the desktop. She needed to deal with this.

When she managed to pick up the phone, she expected to see a familiar number. She expected the rush of disappointment that would certainly come the moment she saw some boring name. It would be another consultant or lawyer, another accountant or programmer. And of course, the caller would expect her to solve a problem.

At some point, she got sick of them.

Then her breath hitched in her lungs. Her throat clenched slightly when she saw that her phone couldn't identify the number.

Her Master.

Sabrina didn't pause. She held the phone to her ear. Voice

quivering, she asked, "Master?"

"Good girl. I was going to punish you for addressing me incorrectly. I'm glad to hear you remember your place."

"Yes, Master. Thank you, Master."

"I have a project for you."

"How can I serve you?"

"First, I want to hear you come for me."

"What?" The question dropped from her lips. Yes, her body still thrummed with desire, but this was her office. It was supposed to a professional sanctum...Despite this, Sabrina recovered. "Yes, Master. How would you like me to do it?"

With every second, she hoped he would change his mind. She silently begged this man. Although he couldn't see her face, he could probably read her tone of voice. He must have known how she felt.

Except he didn't care. Or maybe her reluctance made this even more enticing for him. He could have fun with her. He didn't even need to be in the same room.

"Strip for me."

Sabrina's lips parted a fraction of an inch. She breathed in and out even as her body began to respond to the possibility. From one second to the next, Sabrina couldn't quite tell if this was desire or something else.

"But...but Master...you wouldn't know if I was even really naked."

"You don't think I'll know?"

Sabrina swallowed, genuinely nervous. On the one hand, she didn't think this man had supernatural powers, so if she was alone, then he couldn't tell what she wore. And yet, something in his voice seemed so definite and sure, like there wasn't any question of what needed to happen.

"I'll do it...Sir."

"Good bimbo."

Sabrina gulped again as she stood up. She lowered the phone and turned on the speaker function. From there, she began to strip. She had already been naked once. It seemed she would be nude again, in her office no less. Obedient to her Master, Sabrina unbuttoned her blouse. She unzipped her skirt.

She kicked off her shoes. One layer at a time, she disrobed because a man told her to.

Finally, she took off her bra.

Sabrina glanced back down at her phone. "What, what would you like me to do now, Master?"

"Tell me, how do you feel?"

"Nervous. Ashamed."

"And...?" He clearly discerned something else in her voice.

Sabrina didn't see any alternative. She had to admit the truth, both to this man and to herself. "And I'm horny."

"Yes, you are. That's why you're going to do exactly what I say. Understand, bimbo? I know it's hard for a girl like you. A silly girl. A dumb girl." He teased her, and the heat swirled through her body, but Sabrina didn't dare argue.

"I understand...Master."

"Good."

Silence filled the air, and Sabrina didn't know what to do next. Should she speak? Should she wait? Then it dawned on her. He was messing with her! Just as she tried to summon the courage to speak, his voice buzzed from the phone.

"Get down on your knees. Spread your legs."

Sabrina again reflected on the possibility that she didn't really have to comply. Seriously, he couldn't know. He wouldn't be certain. Even if Cale happened to be a very smart man, he wasn't psychic.

And yet, she walked over to the middle of her office. She slowly got down onto the floor. Resting her weight on the balls of her feet and the tips of her knees, she spread her legs, exposing her pussy.

The air conditioner spalshed cool air all along her body. The chill couldn't come close to conquering the inferno that began to spread through her skin.

"First, I want you to lick your fingertips. Do it slowly."

Sabrina obeyed. She touched her fingertips to her lips, then her tongue. She started to suck on her digits. "Work them into your mouth, slowly. Take your time. Pretend that you're sucking me off again. You did such a good job with that, after all. You should know, slut, I was very impressed with your oral talents. You're a skilled girl. You should be very proud of yourself."

With her fingers in her mouth, she couldn't answer. However, she could grimace ever so slightly. Her Master chuckled, almost like he could guess exactly what expression played along her features.

"Until I tell you otherwise, you aren't allowed to speak."

Sabrina opened her mouth. She instantly meant to answer, to tell him that she understood. Stopping at the last moment, Sabrina managed to stay quiet. At this time, she'd be neither seen nor heard. She'd obey anyway.

"Take your fingertips and play with your right nipple. And remember, if you try to defy me, there are going to be consequences, slut."

Slut. He made her sound dirty and low. Maybe he was right.

Obviously, her Master didn't bother to ask any questions. He didn't inquire to see if she obeyed. He would glean this information all on his own once he had her alone. If she attempted to trick him, there'd be consequences. It was as simple as that, especially when she had a control collar locked around her neck.

For how long?

Sabrina couldn't answer that question. For the moment, she couldn't even ask it.

She massaged her right nipple by his command.

"Now move your hand over to the left side. Touch your nipple gently, just once. I want you to barely caress the tip. Then pull back and stop." Again, she followed his commands. Every word made her feel more and more like some puppet. She didn't think. She simply acted by his commands.

Her Master continued, "I bet you're getting horny. Right now, you're probably getting really eager." He may not have been able to set his eyes on her, but Cale had no problem predicting her movements and feelings.

Somewhere along those lines, she started to nibble down on her bottom lip. Sabrina couldn't help herself.

"Lick your palms," Cale ordered, and she obeyed. She

swiped her tongue over smooth lines of her hands. Next he ordered, "Now massage your naked tits. Do it slowly. Very, very slowly." He let every word hang on the air, each syllable another promise.

Sabrina rested her palms on her naked breasts. Both nipples already glistened with just a hint of salvia. Mouth dry, she stared straight ahead. It didn't help. She couldn't distract herself, nor could this girl hide from the sensations that ran through her skin.

"Remember, slow," he ordered. As the sensations compounded, building into this steady rhythm, he gave her another command. "A little bit faster now. Faster. Build it up. I want you wet. If I walk through those doors, I want to be able to reach between your legs and feel your soaked little slit. I want to touch you and make you shiver. If I let you speak, I want to hear that desperation, slut. You're my little fuck toy and you need to be ready for me. Are you ready?"

Sabrina almost answered. Then she remembered his command. She stopped herself; she froze, holding back those words. It took every ounce of determination she possessed in that tight little body of hers.

"Stop."

The command came from her phone. For a second, she didn't even register the sound. Then this sharp chill stabbed into her. Stop? Really? No. She couldn't. As his chuckles filled the air, Sabrina yanked her hands back from the warm curves of her breasts.

She had barely moved, yet her skin prickled with heat. Her heart kicked in her chest. Every breath of air felt insufficient, like she couldn't fill her lungs all the way, no matter how hard she tried.

And her Master knew it.

"Speak, girl. Tell me what you want."

"I want, I want an orgasm! I want it so badly!"

"Touch yourself, slut. Stroke that little slit of yours. But don't make a sound. Do it now."

Sabrina's hand flew down between her legs. She rested her palm on her pubis. Her palm and wrist moved along her bush, and her fingertips worked deep down. The warm, soft touch got her off fast. A few seconds. Three? Two? Maybe less.

By her Master's command, she stayed silent.

She collapsed onto the floor, and that's when the door opened again.

"You did well," he said to her.

Sabrina didn't really register those words. Crumpled on the floor, she surrendered to the exhaustion. This time around, she had no other choice. Yes, she remained awake, but only in the most technical sense. Her head swam, and she fluttered her eyes every once in a while. But for the most part, this girl just relaxed into her stupor.

Some time later, she awoke.

She opened her eyes and realized she was no longer on the floor. Rather, she found herself on her small couch. She hardly ever paid attention to it. When people visited her office, she had them stand or sit across from her.

Not only had she curled up on the couch, she had pulled a blanket over her naked body?...No, that didn't make any sense. Stretching her limbs, Sabrina sat up and rubbed her eyes.

She found Cale sitting across her desk, his fingers playing along her key board as he typed something in.

"What, what are you doing?"

"Just inputting adding a few programs to your computer."

"Programs?"

"Yes."

Sabrina licked her lips. She was thirsty and hungry and confused. Then she swallowed and she felt the metal around her neck. "Master...would you allow me to take the collar off now?"

"No." He kept his eyes directed back at the screen.

"But..."

"Sabrina, come here."

She started to stand.

"No. Crawl. Like a slave."

Swallowing back her exasperation, Sabrina slipped down onto the floor. She moved along on her knuckles and knees. She stopped just a foot or so away from her Master. "Sabrina, I will remove the collar when I've decided you've had enough time in it. But right now, I don't think you actually want your freedom. No. Do you know what you want?"

"What do I want...Master?" She had to remind herself to use his title.

"You want to stay my slave girl. That's why you're already wet."

Sabrina shook her head. She didn't actually mean to attempt to defy or trick her Master. Rather, she was a modern girl with an inflated sense of her own competence, will, and independence. Whether she could admit it or not, Sabrina still didnt' know a lot about herself.

But her Master did.

"Oh, you don't think you're turned on right now?"

Sabrina opened her mouth. Nothing came out. As hard as she tried, she couldn't come up with the right words to say. Speechless, she squeaked out something adorable and incomprehensible. She made her Master chuckle.

"Stand. Hold your hands behind your back."

It didn't feel good to get back up on her feet, especially naked. Without saying anything else, Cale got out of her seat, and he came up behind her. His fingers went right between her legs.

Damn it! He was right. She was wet, almost drenched. She didn't understand what was wrong with her. How could her body betray her like this? Perhaps it was the hunger, maybe the thirst. Either way, he fingered her gently.

"Want to try that again? Want to tell me you're not a horny slut?"

"I, I can't..." she said, letting those words drift off.

"No, you can't," he said. His hand slipped away from her pussy, and he shoved her forward, bending her across the desk. She hated this position. She gritted her teeth. She didn't even have enough time to figure out what her Master intended.

His hand flew down, smacking into her cute little ass. He savored those sounds, especially when his slut started to moan. Sabrina simply couldn't help herself. He brought her close to an orgasm, only to make her stop and whimper.

"Get dressed," he commanded.

Sabrina whimpered those adorable little noises, but her Master already stepped back. She pushed herself away from the desktop. Facing him, she hoped she might be wrong. With every fiber of her being, she yearned to make an attempt, to try to convince him. But no, she already saw the truth.

"Yes, Master."

Back in her skirt and blouse and shoes, Sabrina stepped out of her office. Relief spread through her body. The office was empty. Even the cleaning crews were gone. She didn't know the exact hour, but no one would see her walk of shame.

Cale came up behind her. He grabbed her shoulder, and he tugged, guiding her back to the elevator. She rode down to the lobby. They went out into the parking lot. It must have drizzled because the ground shone.

Instinctively, Sabrina headed toward her parking spot, but Cale refused to release her. "Where do you think you're going, slave?"

"Home?"

"No," he told her with a slow shake of his head. "But since you're being obstinate and silly, you can ride in my trunk." He had pulled her up to a black sedan. He opened the trunk with the control on his keychain.

When the trunk popped open, she looked down at the space. "You can't be serious." Sabrina crossed her arms over her chest.

"You can go in the trunk in just the collar or I cuff you, punish you, and lock in anyway." He didn't sound angry or offended. This was a simple statement of fact, a set of possibilities, and Sabrina would be the one to make the choice.

"The trunk," she said. She started to climb in. He shoved her, and she landed on her side, just as she had done in her office. That's when he slammed the trunk lid down, encapsulating her in darkness.

A few seconds later, he turned on the engine, and they started driving. At first, she had no problem tracking their progress. He drove out of the parking lot and went right, then left. He stopped at a traffic light, and they waited for several seconds.

Alone in the trunk, Sabrina considered her position. Breathing in and out, she kept searching for some primal fear. Yes, her Master intimidated her, but he didn't scare her. He didn't frighten her because he wouldn't hurt her.

Call it an instinct. Call it an intuition. Either way, she trusted him. As she settled down, Sabrina experienced a different sensation. It crept in slowly. Little by little, the arousal played through her skin, tugging at her concentration. This poor girl couldn't help herself. He teased her, and he used her.

And it just worked her up more and more.

Absurdly, her phone vibrated for her attention.

How is my bimbo? The screen seemed incredibly bright to her. In fact, she had to squint. But she made out that message, and Sabrina didn't know whether or not she was supposed to respond. Even as she held up her device, her thumbs began to move along the screen.

Confused. Why am I in the trunk?

Sabrina waited, and he started driving again. She didn't get an immediate reaction. At the same time, she felt hopelessly lost. She never had a particularly strong sense of direction, but it seemed even weaker now since she couldn't see what was going on.

They came to another stop. It had to be a light, or maybe he simply decided to pull off the road. Either way, her phone buzzed and brightened.

Sabrina, you need to understand that as my bimbo, you'll do whatever I say. Right now, you are my possession. You belong to me.

Sabrina typed out her answer. *Yes, Master.* This time, she had no difficulty imagining him grinning or chuckling.

Clutching her phone, she hoped that there would be another answer soon, but he was driving. She had to wait.

The car came to a stop, and a door opened. Sabrina braced herself, thinking that the trunk would pop up right away. But no, that didn't happen. For one reason or another, her Master wanted her to wait. Maybe they were at a gas station.

Perhaps he had simply pulled off into a parking lot so that he could go buy a hamburger.

Nervous, she closed her eyes, and she waited, listening. She focused her ears on her surroundings, wondering when she would get some kind of answer.

The car door opened and closed a second later, and then the engine turned on again. She grimaced and groaned. She actually hit her hands against the bottom of the trunk, not that it did any good.

They drove some more.

Sabrina knew that he was messing with her. He was toying with her. He wanted her frustrated. He wanted her confused. But this knowledge didn't help. She couldn't just reason away her exasperation. From one second and the next, she had to fight the urge to punch the trunk or to kick out with her feet. It wouldn't do any good, but it might attract her Master's attention. Sabrina didn't want to risk it, lest he decide that she needed some more punishment.

They drove around. She listened to the engine, and she could hear the tires grind against the road beneath them. They drove, and they drove, and they drove. At one point, Sabrina nearly fell asleep, but there was something happening to her.

She should have gotten used to it by now.

She was turned on.

This notion of belonging to a man, of becoming his property, it triggered something within her, and Sabrina couldn't simply ignore it.

At one point, she found her hand sliding back down her body. At the last possible moment, she reminded herself that she shouldn't try to masturbate without permission. No, Sabrina had to be a good girl. She had to wait for her Master to say that it would be okay.

They came to another stop, and she braced herself, thinking that it would just be another game. Faster than she anticipated, the trunk popped open, and her Master reached down. He grabbed her wrist, and he pulled, practically dragging her out of that confined space.

Blinking, she looked around, trying to get her bearings.

They were on a street, surrounded by houses.

They were all quite nice with columns, double doors, and immaculate lawns. Each house seemed to come with a pair of shiny new cars.

"Where, where are we?"

"Come with me, bimbo."

He turned away, and he started walking. Bowing her head down, Sabrina chased after her Master. She followed him up a stone walkway to the porch. He took the steps easily. Sabrina kept wondering what was going on.

"What are we doing here?"

"We are here to work on your training, slut."

She flinched at that final word, especially when it was spoken out here, in this bastion of suburbia. He unlocked the door, and then he pushed it open. Sabrina stepped across the threshold, and she could feel his eyes on her.

This place looked too perfect. From the hardwood floors to the tastefully chosen works of art, it seemed like everything Sabrina could have hoped for in a house. She found herself walking up to one painting in particular. It was done in watercolors, and it emphasized shades of pastel pink, red, and blue.

"This is lovely," she said, turning back around to face her Master.

"I'm glad you approve," he said. "Now get down on your hands and knees."

"Yes, Master," she said in a small voice. She assumed that degraded position, all while Cale circled her. He looked down at her.

"Are you a dirty girl?"

"Yes, Master," Sabrina said, as though there was something in particular she couldn't quite figure out on her own. Did he mean literally or did he simply reference her behavior? Either way, the answer was the same.

"Good," he said.

He started walking, and then he commanded her to follow. He snapped his fingers, and Sabrina crawled along on all fours. She moved along on her knuckles and knees, wondering exactly what he had planned for her. He opened up another door, and he stepped inside, disappearing from the corridor that seemed to run the length of the house.

When she turned right, she saw a large, guest bathroom. It had a big tub and two shower heads. Sabrina didn't know exactly what her Master expected of her, so she waited, still braced on the floor. The marble tiles were cold, and that chill soaked into her limbs.

But Sabrina didn't complain. She knew her place.

"Did you know that collar is waterproof?"

"No, Master. I didn't know that," she told him truthfully.

"Get in," he ordered.

Head bowed, she complied. She followed his wishes as though she didn't have any choice.

He turned on the water, and hot jets flashed down, hitting her skin. Sabrina tried to defend herself, but he grabbed her wrist. Apparently, he didn't care if he got wet. After a few more seconds, her body committed to the shift in temperature.

"That's right. Stand there. Take it."

She blushed, she couldn't tell if the heat radiating along her skin had to do with the degradation or the hot liquid running down her skin. Either way, Sabrina remained in place like a good girl.

As she stared straight ahead, studying the shower's tiled façade, Sabrina didn't notice her Master. He stripped, removing each and every article of clothing. Then he stepped into the shower with her, and he wrapped his arms around her. He pulled her hands behind her back, and he held her like that.

"Sabrina, what do you want?"

"I, I don't know," she said.

"You're going to have to figure it out. Eventually, you're going to have to make a decision," he said to her.

The bimbo slave meant to open her mouth, to ask what this man meant, but then his hand slipped to down between her legs, and he fingered her. As the droplets splashed along her skin, she became overwhelmed.

The sensations crashed into her, making it more and more difficult for this girl to think. Pretty soon, she didn't worry about any questions or answers. On the contrary, she simply experienced those impulses dancing between her nerves. Water and his solidity, heat and blush, and so much more.

He worked her up, and Sabrina braced herself, thinking orgasm would come soon.

"No," he told her, pulling his hand back. Before she could climax, he spanked her. The water made the strike even sharper. The confined space made this sound boom in her eardrums.

"Hands above your head," he commanded. "Close your eyes."

Because he was in the shower with her, Sabrina didn't think that her Master could punish her at this point. And yet, he was bigger and stronger. More to the point, it would be very easy for this man to retrieve his phone. And once he did so, it would be excruciatingly simple for him to discipline her, even at a distance.

So Sabrina moved to the back of the shower. She held up her arms. He touched his hand to her forehead, and he made it clear he wanted her to shut her eyes. Sabrina obeyed like a silly bimbo.

"You know what I love about making you come? It's the same thing I enjoy most about making you horny."

She couldn't be certain she had the answer, yet to Sabrina decided to have a guess. She licked her lips even as beads of water continued to run rivulets along the contours of her tight little frame.

"You like me horny because I can't think. You like me when I'm dumb."

"I was like you, Sabrina," he told her. "But I like you best when you're dumb."

She gritted her teeth, locking her jaw, but it didn't change anything. This man could say whatever he wanted. He could tell her anything, and she had to agree.

She heard something above her head. He touched something to the wall, and Sabrina had to keep her eyes shut. Even when he grabbed her wrists and readjusted them, shifting her position, she still couldn't argue or complain. Then she felt the restraints loop around her wrists.

Wait, that didn't make any sense. Sabrina didn't understand, especially because she had taken in the shower at a glance. She knew there weren't any shackles, yet she tried to pull her arms back down, only to fail.

"Open your eyes," he ordered.

Sabrina obeyed again, and she turned her gaze upward. That's when she saw the suction cup restraints. For just a second, she smirked before dashing that curve of amusement from her lips.

Even so, her Master noticed. "It's okay. Try to pull free. Let's see if you can do it."

This sounded like some sort of trap, but Sabrina decided to make the effort anyway. She pulled on the straps, hoping that she would be able to tear them off. She didn't know why she thought she might succeed here.

At first, she expected it to be easy. After a couple of seconds, nothing happened. The straps gave a tiny bit, perhaps a quarter of an inch, but then they stopped. From there, Sabrina tried harder. She pulled with everything she possessed.

It wasn't enough.

Her Master stood back, watching. He tilted his head to the side. "It's cute when you try," he told her.

Sabrina narrowed her eyes, and she made one more attempt. She tried to pull back, but when she couldn't succeed, he pressed his hands into her breasts. He squeezed them slowly, and she forgot about the restraints. Instead, the arousal came flooding back, washing away all coherent thought.

"You've been a dirty girl. I should probably get you cleaned up," he told her.

His hands, however, kept working along her body. He teased her and touched her, stroking her until she couldn't take any more. And just as the nipple stimulation would have allowed her to climax, he pulled his hands back altogether. He grabbed the bar of soap, and he rubbed it between his hands.

That's when he took the lather and started at her clavicles. His fingertips moved down her body slowly. Every second proved to be tantalizing. Every heartbeat kicked in her chest, yet it still wasn't enough for Sabrina.

When he finally started to rub her tits again, she tried to climax quickly. Apparently, Cale knew exactly what his naughty little bimbo was trying to do. That's why he watched her just long enough to see her almost come.

And then he withdrew his touch, and he smacked her thigh hard.

Sabrina was about to start whimpering when he came in, and he kissed her. Heat from his mouth against her lips made her melt. She was getting close, so incredibly close.

He broke off the kiss, disappointing her again.

As he teased her with those sensations, Sabrina wiggled. She struggled against the shackles holding her to the cool tiles. The water continued to mist out onto the air, but a cold chill spread down her back.

"What should I do with you? How should I play with you?"

"You could kiss me again?"

He reached out, and he took one of her nipples. He pinched it between his finger and his thumb. She hollered out, those sounds coming from her lungs.

"That's what you want."

"Yes, yes, Master!"

"Is this about what you want?"

Sabrina inhaled, she held her breath, and she shook her head. Wet strands of hair clung to her cheeks.

"No, this isn't about what the slave girl wants. This is about how she can please me. Like right now, maybe I should just turn off the water and leave you here for a couple of hours. How would you feel about that, slave?"

"I, I'm not a slave," she insisted.

He grabbed one of her nipples again, he pinched, and he twisted. A sharp a jolt of pain ran through her body, radiating out from that button into the rest of her skin. "You are what I say you are," he told her. "Especially when you wear this." He put one finger to her collar, and he pressed it a little bit harder against the arc of her throat.

Sabrina surrendered. Really, she didn't have any other choice.

"Yes, Master. Whatever you say, Master."

It felt so rewarding and freeing to admit the truth. She told him that she was a slave because she was his property. She was his chattel.

"And what should I do with my little slave?"

"You could use me, Master. Would it please you to use me, Master?"

"Maybe," he said, grabbing some of her hair and tilting her head back. He leaned in, and he kissed her. But this kiss had nothing to do with her desires or her impulses. On the contrary, he only gave her those sensations because he enjoyed the feel of her mouth. As he pressed his body into hers, she could feel his erection. She kept thinking about how it would be when he finally decided to take her.

When he pulled back, Sabrina was panting again. She couldn't quite catch her breath.

"What are you?"

"I'm yours. I'm your slut. I'm your slave. I'm your bimbo!" As she spoke, she could hear her voice begin to crack with desperation.

"Yes, you are." He came up to her, and he pressed his chest into hers. She tried to rub her breasts against his body, but she could hardly move. He pinned her right there, and then his hand was down between her legs. He stroked her inner thighs, starting with the left, then slipping back down to the right. When his hand finally came up to her pussy, Sabrina shivered. She was close, so close to an orgasm.

"May I, may I come?" Sabrina asked, barely able to get out those words.

"No. I want you to think about something, Sabrina. I want you to think about how you can be a good bimbo for me. I want you to tell me exactly what that means."

"It means, it means that I'm dumb! It means that I need you!"

"If you're my bimbo, what you going to care about?"

"Pleasing you, Master!" Sabrina almost wanted to stop herself. But she couldn't, not while he still had his hand between her legs. He played with her, and he toyed with her, working her up. Every second brought a new wave of sensation, another ripple of desire flowing through her body. He knew exactly how to tease her. Every time he touched her, he learned a little bit more.

He was becoming an expert.

"Obviously, you want to please your Master. But how does a bimbo do that?"

Cheeks scrunched her eyes closed, she dipped her head down, and she tried to think. He touched her a little bit harder, a little bit faster, and the desires almost overwhelmed her.

But then, she looked back up at him.

"By thinking about clothes and makeup! By making myself pretty for you!"

"That's right. Nothing is more important than looking good for your Master, isn't that right?"

"Yes!"

He put his hands on her wrists, and he pulled himself forward. Sabrina spread her legs, and she realized something just then. Her Master had positioned her perfectly. When he came forward, he had no problem sliding his cock up against her opening. She kept her ankles as far apart as she could, and then she closed her eyes as he raised himself up. He pushed into her, one hard thrust filled her in less than a second.

Sabrina was already so hot and wet that he had no trouble with her. Even when she clenched down, she was just tight around his circumference.

"Thank you, thank you, thank you, Master!"

"Good girl," he told her. He held her there the shower, and the water washed against his back. He pushed into her, deeper. He filled her up until he buried his cock. Then he pulled back again, only to thrust forward deeper and faster. Her body shook. She couldn't move from the back of the shower, yet he kept going, working her harder and faster. She surrendered to that frenzy, and he forced her to climax, once, twice, three times.

Sabrina lost all track of time, all track of her location. Everything became fuzzy and distorted while he used her. And then he started to climax himself, and she could feel that shuddering deep in her body.

With a grunt, he finished with her. Her Master pulled back, and he turned off the water.

"Have you learned something?"

"Yes!"

"What have you learned?"

"I, I've learned that I need to stop thinking about unimportant things. I need to think about my hair and my makeup! I need to think about being a good girl for you."

He got out of the shower, and when he came back, he had a razor.

"You know what I expect of you."

Sabrina took the razor, and she stared down at it. Then her gaze drifted down to her pussy...he wanted her to shave off her pubic hair. He wanted to alter her body, to make sure that she fit his needs and desires.

"Yes...Yes, Master."

As the water continued to shoot down into the shower stall, Sabrina held onto the blade. She peered down between her legs.

Back in college, one of Sabrina's friends complained about this. She went on and on about how men didn't really want women. They didn't really want to be with actual adults. Oh no. Men craved young girls, naked and bare of any real hair. This way, the girls wouldn't question their men. They'd be good and docile. They'd do as they were told.

With a collar around her neck, Sabrina smirked ever so slightly as she wondered what that friend would say about her current situation.

Shrugging off those thoughts and worries, Sabrina took the razor and she slid it along her skin. Little by little, she shaved off her pubic hair. Her movements were slow and steady. She was very careful.

As she finished, Sabrina set aside the blade, and she looked back down at her mound. She was smooth. For a few seconds, she couldn't actually believe it. Wasn't she supposed to be better than this? Wasn't she supposed to be smart enough to make her own decisions?

"No." She whispered that single syllable, and she giggled.

When she emerged from the bathroom, she glanced down the hallway. She held onto a towel as she continued to dab the different spots of her body. "Master?" called the bimbo. "Master, where are you?" Her voice rose a tiny bit as she took in her new surroundings.

She passed several art prints. A black and white tsunami. A colorless ball of fire, like some sort of black sun. Sabrina didn't know if she could read anything from those images. Perhaps they said something about her Master's personality. Maybe not.

Coming back into the living room, she found Cale sitting there. He had a tablet in hand as he considered some article or image.

"Kneel."

"Yes, Master," Sabrina replied quickly, dropping down before this man. She dipped her head low, and she gazed at the floor.

"How are you feeling?"

"Nervous. Horny."

"I'm sure you are." The corners of his mouth rose. "I do find it amazing how often you seem to feel that particular mixture. Tell me, slut, how long do you think it'll take before you get used to your new life?"

Sabrina gulped. For a second, she hoped her Master didn't pick up on the sound of her trepidation. The corners of his mouth rose again, promising he had. "I...I don't know."

"Sabrina, I need to do some more work," he told her. He lowered the zipper on his fly again. Their eyes met, and Sabrina licked her lips. At the same time, she didn't know what to do. Should she approach her Master? Did he expect her to wait for an invitation.

Ultimately, she decided to do the best she could. "Master, how may I please you?"

"Smart girl," he said with a chuckle. More seriously, he added, "We're going to have to work on that."

"Work on what, Master?" She blinked at him, doing her best to appear as vacant as possible, like she couldn't possibly guess what he was thinking.

But this was Cale. He knew how to read this young woman. He'd been studying her for weeks, all while she barely noticed him. "Work on making you a stupid bitch," he told her. He patted her on the head, and then he said, "Go ahead. Suck me off. I know you want to."

She did.

As inexplicable as it seemed, Sabrina couldn't help herself. Something about the degraded position, the sensation of carpet on her knees, the heat and feel of his shaft in her mouth...Sabrina craved it.

She crawled forward and lifted herself up. Then she placed her knees on the carpet, and she started with one lick at the base of his shaft. "That's right," he said. Clearly, he enjoyed that darting little movement.

So Sabrina gave him another. She slipped her tongue to that spot right between his balls and his dick. She licked up along the length of his manhood. By the third sweep of her tongue, Sabrina risked a glance up at her Master.

Their eyes met.

He was smiling at her. She froze, wondering if perhaps she had made some sort of mistake. But then he nodded for her to keep going. Parting her lips, she leaned forward a bit more.

"This is where you belong, Sabrina. This is what you are," he told her. "You're my private little slut, my little human sex toy. Just keep sucking. You don't need to say anything." Lifting her eyes again, she nonetheless stared back at him. "Tonight, you're going to make a call. You'll let that secretary of yours know that you won't be able to make it to work for the next few days."

This had to be a test. Her eyes flickered and she nearly choked. Somehow, sucking off this man by his command didn't faze her. It turned her on, but she could cope. The notion of missing work? That shocked the bimbo.

Just as she attempted to slide her head back, he grabbed Sabrina by her russet strands. He gripped her tight, sending a spasm of pain running through her scalp. She could whimper, but she couldn't speak, not with a dick in her mouth. He forced her head down. She took inch after inch of his shaft into her mouth.

"Listen to me. You want to be my bimbo? Fine. You want to be my slut? Okay. You want to become my mindless little fuck toy?" As he talked down to her, Sabrina grimaced, she blushed, and she got hot. The wetness gathered between her legs, another reminder of what this man could do to her.

Every question already came with an answer. "You want to be mine? Suck. Suck, slut."

Sabrina obeyed. As he set the tempo, she hollowed her cheeks. She pulled gently, her lips tight around this cock. Sabrina kept licking even as she sucked. Her tongue darted and played around his tip, then his length, and back to his tip again. She worshipped him until he yanked hard on her mane.

Pulled away from his shaft, Sabrina sputtered.

"Do you have anything you want to say, slut?"

Her eyes watered. She kept them downcast. She wondered what he would do with her...or to her. "I'll make the call, Master."

"And how will you sound?"

"Cheerful?"

"Yes. And?"

"Happy?"

"Yes. And?"

"Like an airhead? Like a bimbo?"

"That's right," he told her. He stood up, and he grabbed her hair in one hand again. Sabrina didn't bother trying to stand. If her Master wanted her on her feet, then he'd give her the command.

With his bimbo on her knees, he reached down and touched his fingers to the base of his cock. "Open up," he commanded.

For a second, Sabrina didn't understand what he had planned, not until he grazed his fingers along the base of his erection. His fingers played over that sensitive spot.

Sabrina closed her eyes. She parted her lips as she awaited the deluge.

"Eyes open," he commanded.

It took her a second, but Sabrina managed. His manhood was right there, wet and shining with her saliva. Sabrina knew what would happen next, but she didn't know how to brace herself. Instinctively, she tried to turn her head to the side. Her Master wouldn't allow it. He tugged on her hair, sending another dart of pain down into her scalp.

He squeezed at his base, he raised his head, and he gave in. He embraced the pleasure as it shot through him, one throbbing pulse at a time. In those seconds, he shot his load straight onto his bimbo's face.

Sabrina kept her eyes and mouth open. The first squirts hit her cheek. His orgasm splashed a little bit lower. Redirecting his focus, he looked down at her, and he aimed. He blasted his come into her mouth and over the tip of her tongue.

"You like that, don't you?"

She stared back up at him as she tasted those dregs. Excitement burned over her skin, but this wasn't enough.

When he finished, he slid his cock back into his pants. He pulled up his zipper, and he sat down again.

Sabrina didn't say anything. She licked her lips clean, but she didn't touch the rest of his load. Did she feel dirty? Yes. Did she feel like a slut? Absolutely. But if her Master wanted her to pay attention to something more, then she needed to wait for his next command.

"Would my slut like an orgasm?"

"Yes, Master," she said, her voice slow and meek, just the way he liked.

"Then spread your legs and touch yourself. You have one minute," he explained to her.

Sabrina blinked, confused. She had a time limit?

"The clock's ticking," he promised her as he sat back down and picked up his tablet. He went back to his article. In the meantime, Sabrina knew that his eyes would drift back up to the clock at the top of his screen.

Scrambling through her nerves and excitement, Sabrina fell down onto her back. She spread her legs, she closed her eyes, and she pushed her fingers back down to her pussy.

Each second ticked against her. She enjoyed the luxury of a slow breath as her fingers began to move a slow, calming rhythm. The pleasure expanded, rippling out through her body.

The tension built, and Sabrina started to go faster. She nibbled on the inside of her mouth as she experienced that paradox of sensation. She relaxed away from the stresses of her life as a different sort of tension mounted between her nerves.

"What are you going to do?"

"I'm going to skip work, Master."

"Yes, you are."

He reached down, he cupped her chin, and he forced her to look back into his face. This man should have been just another consultant, a man in a suit. He should have been a random piece of information. But in that moment, she felt the totality of his ownership.

The pleasure flared through her body, this snap of ecstasy. She gasped, she surrendered, and she lost all control.

A few minutes later, Sabrina made the call.

Chapter 8

"Sabrina...wake up, Sabrina...Sabrina...It's time to get up."

Those words nudged at her psyche, yet some part of her rebelled. She was warm and comfortable. She felt so small and safe under those sheets. For the first time in a very, very long time, Sabrina didn't think about work or assignments. She didn't have any tasks at all hovering at the back of her mind, demanding her attention.

It felt...so wonderful.

"Sabrina," came that voice again, alluring in its own way.

Ever since middle school, Sabrina had forced herself to wake up with an alarm. Every day. Even weekends. She never wanted to mess around. Every day had to be a battle between her own ambitions and the limits of her body.

This time there was no alarm, just that voice. He whispered to her again, "Sabrina, it's time for you to get up..."

"Yes...Master," whispered the bimbo as she rolled over.

She had spent the night in a guest room, and now her owner was seated at the foot of the bed. As her eyes fluttered open, Sabrina stretched her arms. "Master?" she asked as some of the old trepidation crept back.

"What is it, bimbo?"

She shivered at that word. No matter how many times he called her that, he provoked a response. It was biological.

Doing her best to focus, she rubbed her eyes and looked back at him. He had showered and shaved. "What will you do with me today? I called in sick last night. My employees won't worry about me."

"You want an assignment? Is that it?"

"Yes, Master."

"Get dressed. There are clothes in the closet."

That command should have been easy for a bright girl like Sabrina to follow. But as he headed out of the room, he paused and told her, "Wear something dirty. Pick out a dress or shorts that'll make you feel like you've lost something when you put them on."

Blush played along her cheeks and up to the contours of

her ears. She understood exactly what he intended for her. More to the point, he lifted up his phone.

This command had been programmed and entered into her collar.

Once he left the room, Sabrina rolled out of bed. The morning air was cool, but not unpleasantly so, against her naked skin. A few goose bumps appeared over her shoulders as she padded her way to the closet.

Dirty. She had to wear something *dirty.*

Sabrina had never played with clothing, not like some of the other women she had known. Starting in seventh grade, she noticed how some of the other girls focused almost entirely on what they wore. And even if those girls couldn't or wouldn't admit it, their choices always had to impress the boys.

Maybe it would be a pleated skirt, tight shorts to show off her pert little ass, maybe it would be jeans embroidered with flowers along the legs. No matter the exact choice, those clothes would make the girl feel better or stronger, somehow more powerful or complete.

Not Sabrina.

She did a reasonably good job of picking out her attire. She would wear loose jeans or wear shirts when it was cold.

Sabrina took several steps forward, and she found herself surrounded by clothing.

"Master?"

Cale walked right by her, and he reached out, sliding his fingers through hers. He held on tight, and he tugged gently, guiding her deeper and deeper into the store.

Sabrina had driven by this boutique many times, yet she never stopped and considered what might be contained inside. It just seemed so normal, so average...Besides, Sabrina was a kind of girl who tended to do most of her shopping online.

Officially, she enjoyed the efficiency. She liked the fact that she didn't have to work hard at getting what she wanted.

"Hello," said a woman behind a desk right there in the middle of the store. "How can I help you?"

"I would like you to help my girl here."

"Okay, let me see what I have to work with. Let me see, let me see."

At first, Sabrina didn't know how to react to this woman. She had blonde hair that fell down around her face, flirting with the edges of her shoulders. Not only that, she had on pink mascara, bright red lipstick, and she wore a cotton candy colored jacket over a pale blue corset along with a pleated skirt. When the woman came out from behind her desk, she revealed that she wore a pair of pink high heels.

"Master?" Sabrina asked, tugging on her owner's grip.

Cale didn't answer, not right away. Instead, he pulled her a little bit closer, and he tilted Sabrina's head to the side. He whispered down to her. "I know this is going to be difficult, but I don't mind. You see, you need to learn how to be a good girl. You need to learn how to become an obedient bimbo. This girl is going to help you with that."

"She looks like an airhead."

"She is an airhead," her Master agreed. "And that's the entire point. She knows how to do this. You, however, do not. So are you going to be a good girl for me?"

"What, what is this place?" Sabrina said that question loud enough that both her Master and this strange woman heard easily.

"My name is Kylie, and this is my shop. Well, it actually belongs to my owner, but I work here most of the time."

Sabrina looked back at the other woman, and that's when she noticed of the collar around Kylie's neck. It matched Sabrina's perfectly.

"You've been trained. You are a bimbo."

"Bimbo, slut, slave," Kylie agreed. She held her hands behind her back, and she gave a little hop. "I'm a happy girl because I know my place!"

"What, what's going to happen now?" Sabrina asked.

Kylie glanced back at Cale, almost like she expected him to speak first because he was the de facto authority figure here. He was, after all, a man.

"You're going to spend the rest of the day here with Kylie. She's going to tell you what to do and how to behave, and you are going to obey her. If you don't, there will be consequences."

"Like I get to punish you!" Kylie called out. She gave another little hop.

Sabrina didn't know how this girl could possibly achieve those kinds of movements, especially while she had on those high heels.

Turning back to her master, Sabrina started to shake her head. "How, how does she get to punish me?"

This time, Sabrina didn't wait. She grabbed up a phone from her desk, and she touched her thumb to the screen. All of a sudden, an electrical jolt flashed through Sabrina's body, knocking her off balance. She hit the floor, landing on her knees.

Kylie walked up to her, and she bent forward. "You see, you need to be trained. You need to be bimbofied, and that's why I'm here. My owner and your Master are friends, so they both trust me. Isn't that lovely?" She spoke with an insipid giggle in her voice, like every word was so cheerful!

"I, I can't stay here!" Sabrina said. She pushed herself back up onto her feet, and she started walking. She marched back toward the door, but another blast of pain shot through her body, starting at her neck and emanating down through the rest of her skin.

Sabrina collapsed again. She hit the floor, hard.

"No one said you could go," Kylie called out with another little giggle. "It's okay. As soon as you learn to do as you're told, I'm sure will be the best of friends! Maybe we will even be able to put on a little show for our owners."

Sabrina turned back to Cale. "Master, please don't do this. Please, don't make me stay here!"

He came up to her, and Sabrina remained down on her knees. He touched two fingers to the underside of her chin. "Bimbo, do you remember why you put the collar on in the first place?"

Eyes wet, Sabrina couldn't force herself to speak. She couldn't make a sound. "You put the collar on because you needed someone to control you. You needed to be reduced and degraded. It's what you crave more than anything else. And now you're going to get it. Yes, you are," he told her.

Surprisingly, Cale crouched down for just a moment. He reached up Sabrina skirt, and he fingered her panties. Her excitement had already dampened her underwear. "That's what I thought," he said, and then he got up and left her there.

Sabrina remained on her knees, watching as her Master left. Distantly, she picked up on the sounds of Kylie's footsteps.

"So what do we have here?" Kylie asked. The blonde girl started to circle, almost like a predator inspecting some potential prey.

Under normal circumstances, Sabrina would not have allowed a woman like Kylie to intimidate her, especially considering what the blonde doll on. She looked like some slutty toy.

But here and now, knowing full well that this girl could shock and punish her, Sabrina didn't know how to answer.

"I think we have a girl who still wants to be independent. I think we have a girl who doesn't realize how much it sucks to try to think for herself." Assuming the same position Cale had maintained only a few minutes before, she touched Sabrina under her chin, forcing her to lift her gaze.

"Are you a smart girl? Is that what you want to be?"

Sabrina shook her head.

"Say it."

Sabrina opened her mouth, but then she couldn't make a sound. That's when Kylie lifted up the remote control. The other girl just wasn't fast enough, so Kylie had no problem pressing the button once again, delivering another painful shock.

"You, you didn't need to do that!" By this point, Sabrina had collapsed forward. Inhaling and exhaling, she held herself up on her hands and knees.

"Sure, I did!" Kylie chirped back at the other girl. "You still don't understand. You still think that you are a smart girl. You aren't. You're dumb. You're a dumb bimbo, and that's why you needed it."

This time, Sabrina didn't say anything. She stared down at the linoleum floor.

"Fine. Whatever. What's next?" Sabrina started to stand.

Kylie delivered another electrical shock. The blast shot through Sabrina's body, lighting up the pain receptors in her neck and down her chest. She flinched, and she whimpered. She fell back down, there was nothing she could do about it.

"If you want to get up, you need to ask for permission."

"Hey, you think I'm just a dumb bimbo. Doesn't that mean you're dumb bimbo to?"

"I am your teacher! I get to tell you what to do!" Kylie sounded so pleased with herself, like this was incredibly wonderful.

It wasn't fair. Even so, Sabrina didn't say anything.

"Now, would you like to get back up? Would you like to stand so that we can get started on your wardrobe?"

"What's wrong with my wardrobe?"

"Obviously, you don't look slutty enough," Kylie replied. She flashed another big, happy smile. "When your owner sees you, he should always know that you are ready and willing to do whatever he wants. You need to be horny all the time, and your clothing should express that!" She actually clapped her hands together, like this was something new and wonderful.

Sabrina locked her teeth together. "Can I please get up?"

"Only because you asked so nicely," Kylie answered. She stepped back, almost like she expected Sabrina to leap at her, to try to grab the phone from her grip. That was probably wise.

Sabrina pushed herself back up onto her feet.

"Now, hold your hands behind your back so that I can get a really good look at you. I need to evaluate you to see how we can make you better for your owner."

"Did you sign up for this too?"

"Why do you want to know?"

Sabrina may have parted her lips, but she stopped a second later. She knew this question would get her in trouble, so she froze up. She refused to say anything else. Unfortunately for her, Kylie wasn't about to let it go.

"Tell me. What were you about to ask?" Kylie smirked ever so slightly with just one corner of her mouth rising a tiny bit.

"Nothing."

"Are you sure about that?"

With her eyes down, Sabrina didn't see the other woman lift up the phone. She didn't realize that Kylie's finger hovered just above the screen, ready to press the command. In another moment, pain flashed through her body. The signal jumped from the phone to the collar, and of the electrodes jolted her with another burst of pain.

Sabrina hissed. She hissed and nearly fell forward again. It took all of her self-control to remain upright.

"Try that again," Kylie ordered, her voice just as cheerful and energetic as before.

"I, I wanted to know if you were a bimbo before you put the collar around your neck."

"Oh, no. I was a very intelligent young woman."

"I doubt that," Sabrina replied. She braced herself, locking her teeth together because she expected another rush of pain. It didn't arrive. On the contrary, Kylie started giggling again. "You really are a very silly girl. You don't know anything about how this works."

"What, what do you mean?"

"You're Master wants me to help you become a bimbo. He knows that you don't really get it. But in a little while, you will. You'll start to understand how this actually works."

"I still, I still don't understand," Sabrina replied, doing her best to keep the edge of frustration out of her voice. After all, she despised the idea that this woman knew more about anything than her.

"Strip for me."

Swallowing, Sabrina began to obey. Her Master had given her that order many times before. It made sense that Kylie would want to see her naked. Despite the trembling her fingers, Sabrina obeyed. She started to pull off her garments, one at a time.

Because of her obedience, it seemed that Sabrina was going to get an answer. Kylie circled the other woman. "When we think about the life of a bimbo, it probably seems really easy, especially to the guys who want us. From their perspectives, we are just dumb girls. And that's true. As a bimbo, you don't really think about world events or high finance or physics. You aren't smart in that sense, but that's okay. Because you're going to be happy!"

"I still don't understand," Sabrina grumbled.

"That's because I'm not done explaining it to you, silly. Be quiet and listen like a good girl. I know I'm not your Master, but I still have his authority, so you need to be quiet when I talk. Isn't that right?"

Again, Sabrina hated acknowledging this woman's superiority, yet she had no choice. "Yes," she said in a small, almost timid tone.

After one more giggle, Kylie kept going. Sabrina was now down to her bra and panties. "As a bimbo, you still need to think about what is going to please your Master. You still need to figure out what is going to make him happy. And he's a person, so he evolves. Sure, some of the stuff is very basic. When he walks through the door, he might expect a blow job or a foot massage. You obviously have to cook and clean for him, but you can't just do the same thing every single day. You need to adapt. You need to evolve. You need to think about exactly what it'll take to be a good girl for him."

"Why would anyone sign up for this?" Sabrina muttered, almost whispering. She took off her bra. She only had on her panties now, yet her pussy remained a damp. Even through her confusion, she couldn't think of a good answer. She couldn't think of some reasonable response.

"You already know the truth. Tell me." Kylie cupped Sabrina's cheek in her hand.

"I, I don't know!"

"Are you sure about that?" Kylie asked, sliding her hand down into Sabrina's panties. The other girl started to touch and fondle and finger Sabrina. The former CEO couldn't do anything about it. After all, Kylie still had the phone in her other hand. With just a tap, she could send another blazing jolt of agony through Sabrina's body.

Realizing this, Sabrina stood there. Not only that, she actually widened her stance, make it even easier for Kylie to touch her. That young woman with her deft little fingers continued to play with Sabrina's pussy.

"You know exactly why you want this. You know exactly what you need. Tell me, Sabrina, and then we can get started on your makeover."

Closing her eyes, Sabrina inhaled and exhaled. She gasped through the anticipation running through her body. She could feel those tingles along the pads of her fingertips. She could feel it in the arches of her feet, in her core, everywhere. It even felt like her lips were sparkling with this fresh desire.

"I, I want to be a bimbo because I don't want to think about myself anymore. I don't want to plan for the future. I just want to be dumb and grateful!"

"That's right!" Kylie chirped, speeding her fingers up. "You want to have a man who will tell you what to do. You'll take care of him, and he will make sure that you always know your place. He'll make sure that you're safe, you don't have to stress, you just get to blink and obey. Because that's what you really want, isn't it, Sabrina? You just want to be dumb and grateful. It's what you need. It's what we all need."

The ecstasy exploded through Sabrina's body, and she collapsed down onto her knees once again.

It took several seconds, but on her vision finally cleared, Sabrina lifted her head, and she looked back up at her tutor. "I, I think I understand now." Her face was hot, and her thoughts still seemed scattered, but at least she got that sentence out there.

"You're getting closer," Kylie corrected.

"Come on," Kylie said a few moments later. She started to walk away, deeper into the store.

That's when Sabrina blushed brightly, glancing back at the doorway. She forgot that this was a public shop, that anyone could stroll into this boutique at any moment. Bright with shame, Sabrina scurried after the other woman.

Kylie took Sabrina down a narrow hallway. Then she turned sharply into another room. There was a sink, a chair, and several shelves adorned with different kinds of hair care products. Sabrina didn't recognize most of them.

"What, what are we doing here?"

"Don't be nervous. You know that I'm going to take care of you. You know that you don't have a choice anyway. So why get frightened at all?"

"I've always taken a lot of pride in my hair," Sabrina said. And that was true. In virtually every aspect of her life, she tried to be efficient. But when it came to her hair, she had no problem spending extra money or waiting weeks on end to meet with the right stylist.

"That's good. And you're going to keep doing that as a blonde."

"What?" Sabrina shrieked. She tried to pull away, to run back toward the exit. After all, she already knew how this game would play out. So long as Kylie had that controller, she could compel any kind of response she wished.

"You're going to be a blonde. All bimbos are blonde!"

Sabrina kept going, racing back toward the exit, only to feel the familiar blast of electricity. She stumbled forward, throwing her arms up against in the doorway for balance. Kylie grabbed her, and she brought the other girl back over to the chair. She pushed the naked girl down, and then she touched her palm to Sabrina's forehead.

"I don't want to punish you again, but I will if you try to get up. This is going to happen, Sabrina. Just let it happen. You know this is what you want. You don't want people to take you seriously. You want them to see you and to know the truth. You want to be on the outside what you are on the inside."

Glowering, Sabrina refused to acknowledge any of those points.

"Don't worry. I know exactly what I'm doing!"

Sabrina didn't respond.

"Just relax. This is going to be easy."

Sabrina still didn't answer, but she didn't try to pull away, not even when Kylie nudged her head down toward the sink. Kylie rolled up her sleeves, and she began to dampen Sabrina's hair. The water was warm, and the other girl's fingertips against her scalp actually felt really good.

Even so, Sabrina's heart kept thundering in her chest with one simple fact. Her hair was about to be changed. It would be dyed, turning her into a blonde.

From one second into the next, Sabrina tried to figure out what this would mean for her. She didn't have an easy answer.

"Just relax. That's right. Close your eyes. You know this feels good. You know you don't want to really think about anything."

Kylie's breathless tones made it easy for Sabrina to slide her eyelids down. She relaxed, and she surrendered it to the weight of her body. She already knew that this would happen one way or another.

She could struggle and fight, but she would lose. Or she could just stay right there, trusting that her Master knew what he was doing. He put her in Kylie's hands; Sabrina had no choice but to trust him.

Kylie continued to work.

Sabrina didn't know how much time had gone by. But finally, it was time for the unveiling. Still naked, Sabrina kept her eyes closed until Kylie positioned her exactly where she wanted her.

"Ready?"

"Yes," whispered Sabrina. She didn't know she was lying at that point, yet it didn't seem to matter.

Hours had gone by, and Sabrina had experienced that strange paradox of boredom and nervous tension. But now, she waited, wondering exactly how she would look. When people saw her again, what would they think of her? Would they still respect her? Or would they automatically assume she had to be an airhead?

Sabrina considered her first impression of Kylie. For all Sabrina knew, Kylie had been some brilliant young woman, only to become dumb and eager. At first glance, however, she seemed so silly, like she couldn't possibly have a good idea of her own.

Wrinkling her lips together, Sabrina waited. "I'm ready," she said again.

"Open your eyes," Kylie commanded, and Sabrina obeyed, if only tentatively.

She looked back at her reflection, and her breath caught in her throat.

It was worse than she expected. It was worse than she could have possibly imagined. Sabrina found herself looking back at her image, except her dark brown tresses were bright blonde. She looked completely different now.

"Your eyes match," Kylie announced. "You are a blue-eyed, blonde haired pretty girl. All of the guys are going to see you, and are not going to listen to a word you have to say. They're going to want to touch you here," Kylie announced, cupping one of Sabrina's breasts. "And here," said the girl, squeezing Sabrina's ass. "And don't forget down here," Kylie finished, running her fingers down toward Sabrina's smooth pubis.

"Lovely, but now we need to work on your wardrobe."

"I was already dressed like a slut."

"Honey, dressing like a slut involves more than just putting on something short or tight. You need to do better than that if you want to please your Master!"

Sabrina's hair was still wet, but Kylie grabbed her by the hand and pulled, practically yanking her back through the hallway.

As far as Sabrina knew, the door remained unlocked. And yet, they were back in the boutique, standing between the different racks of clothing.

"Pick something out, something that you think will please your owner."

Sabrina quickly scanned through the shop, searching for different possibilities. When she started moving, she didn't think. Instead, she just grabbed a pair of white stockings, a short pink skirt, a purple halter top, and some panties. She didn't think about it. No, Sabrina just wanted to cover herself.

Once she gathered everything up, she started to put it on it.

Kylie walked right over to her, and she knocked the garments out of Sabrina's hands.

"No. No. No. That isn't how you do it."

"You told me to pick out some clothes. That's exactly what I did!" Sabrina didn't even notice the way that her voice started to sound just a little bit whiney. She sounded more like an airhead.

"I did. But I also told you to do a good job."

"I don't understand!" Sabrina couldn't believe it, but she actually stamped her foot down against the floor. She was acting like a child, but she couldn't quite help herself.

Sabrina wanted to put something on. That's when she realized what she needed to do. "Can you dress me?"

"I'd be happy to," Kylie replied happily. She started to scurry around, and whenever Sabrina tried to move from her spot, Kylie would just lift her hand and wag her finger. "No. No. Stay right where you are." With a look of exasperation on her pretty face, Sabrina wouldn't see any other alternative. She had to stand there and wait, wondering what Kylie would do for her.

Finally, Kylie finished, and she came back with a taffeta skirt. It was red with little plaid designs running along the sides. Then she held out a long sleeved sweatshirt adorned with a blue bow across the front.

"That doesn't look very slutty," Sabrina said, and she didn't know whether or not she was even complaining.

"Being a slut doesn't necessarily mean just showing off more skin. You can do that whenever you want. Your Master will probably make you do it every day, but he should be able to show you off. Being a good bimbo means doing whatever it takes to please your Master. So right now, you're going to put all of this on. Oh, and you'll need these," Kylie said, grabbing a pair of high heels.

Sabrina hated high heels, but she knew better than to try to complain or argue. She slid her feet down into those dainty pieces, and she felt the shift in her balance.

"Walk across the room for me."

"I can't. It feels like I'm walking on stilts!"

"Too bad. Try." Kylie offered up a silent reminder by lifting up the phone. It would be so easy for her to push the screen, to send the signal.

Swallowing back her trepidation, Sabrina started to walk forward.

She made her way along the floor, and she could feel her steps wobble along. She couldn't believe that she was doing this. She couldn't believe that she had on this short little skirt. Her panties were easily on display.

As her breath quivered in her chest, Sabrina stopped.

"Back straight. You want to make sure that your breasts are on easy display for your owner and any of his friends. You always want to remember that you are an accessory. Your job is to make your Master look good!" Kylie called out.

Narrowing her eyes, Sabrina didn't know if she could tolerate this. But again, she forced herself to start walking. It required all of her concentration to simply maintain her balance.

When she made it back to Kylie, Sabrina was practically panting, as though she had run a marathon.

"No do that five more times."

"What? I can't!"

"This is all part of your training," Kylie explained, making it sound so simple and easy. "Go ahead. Get started."

Sabrina couldn't believe that she was taking orders from this girl. And yet, she started to mince her way across the floor. She held out her hands for balance, and it helped a little bit. Her confidence started to build.

"There you go. You see, you're doing it! This isn't so hard. Just relax and concentrate on what you want to do. Clear your mind of everything except pleasing your owner."

"You aren't my owner."

Kylie giggled again. "No, of course I'm not your owner. Your owner is a big, handsome, strong man. But he told me to train you, so that's exactly what we're doing. Just a couple more laps. Come on. You can do it!"

Sabrina hated the encouragement. It made her feel absurd, yet she kept going. She worked her way across the floor, moving to and fro just as Kylie demanded.

When she finally came to a stop, Kylie looked back at the girl. "Nice. Now we can work on your makeup!"

Sabrina gave a curt nod. Yes. Sure. Whatever. After another second, she started to reach down, hoping that she would get to take off the heels.

"No. No. Those stay on!"

"But they're so uncomfortable!"

"You'll get used to them," Kylie said, patting Sabrina on the head. "Sometimes you need to suffer a little bit to be gorgeous for your owner."

When Sabrina didn't answer, Kylie accepted that as acquiescence. The two girls went back into the hallway, and Kylie took Sabrina into another dressing room. There were several lights, a big mirror, and a small desk. Sabrina sat down, and then the next lesson began.

For nearly an hour, Kylie lectured. She talked about foundations, blushes, different colors, and of the best way to pout.

"The pout is very important. You see, when you pout out your lips, it tells your Master that you are interested in sex. And that's always important. You're a horny girl, so you need to make sure that your owner will always remember that you are available and eager. The pout is part of that."

"My Master just puts his hand down my panties."

"Mine does that too!" Kylie called out with another simpering giggle. "It's like we're sisters!"

Sabrina glared back at her reflection, especially now. She had on way too much makeup. She really did feel like a slut, like she was just some girl out to go snag some male attention. She didn't care how it happened, so long as someone would focus on her.

"Now, are you ready to go out?"

"Go out?"

Kylie put her hands on her hips. "Absolutely. There's a lunch downtown with some of my friends. We need to see what you've learned. We need to see if you can be a good bimbo in public. That's going to be a really important part of your training!"

"I, I can't go out, not like this!"

Sabrina just turned her attention back down to her absurdly short skirt. The idea of stepping out into public like this sent chills running through her body. And yet, there was something else, this hint of desire racing along her body as well.

Before she could really think about it, there was that special trace of warmth right between her legs.

"You can, and you will! Trust me, you just want to be a good bimbo. You don't want me to have to take you out on a leash. That would be very, very embarrassing for a girl like you."

"You wouldn't dare!"

With another silly grin, Kylie just giggled out, "Try me!"

No, Sabrina couldn't do it. With a sigh, she agreed.

In a short skirt and her bow-sweater, Sabrina stepped into the restaurant. Kylie was several steps ahead already. It was lunch, just as the other girl had announced. At this point, Sabrina was hungry, yet her trepidation kept swirling through her body.

Sabrina didn't know what to expect, but she could already feel something.

Attention.

There were lots of young executives out and about. They were conducting business, making deals, or flirting with some of the servers. Maybe those same executives, every one a young man, needed to get out to enjoy some freedom away from the office.

With her heels clicking against the floor, Sabrina did her best to keep up with Kylie. But Kylie was practiced. She knew how to glide through the larger room even in those high heels. For her part, Sabrina needed to concentrate. She had to hold out her arms, almost like she walked a tightrope.

"Everyone, I want you to meet Sabrina. She is going to be the newest bimbo in town." Kylie had stopped at a round table with several other young women. They were all blonde. They were all dressed like sluts, and they all giggled. A lot.

Sabrina looked around the table, and she could hardly believe it. How could these women take themselves seriously? But then she recalled her own reflection, and she knew exactly how she looked.

"Sabrina, meet the girls. This is Mandy. This is Candy. This is Tabby, and this is Gabby. Oh, and those two girls are Taylor and Skyler." Sabrina turned her attention back to those last two, and she couldn't help but blink with surprise.

Taylor and Skyler looked like they were sisters, maybe even twins!

Sabrina opened her mouth to say something, but Kylie yanked on her wrist, forcing Sabrina to sit down.

Within the span of just a few seconds, all of the other girls started chatting and talking. They were laughing and telling jokes. Sabrina did her best to follow along, but it sounded like all they talked about was makeup, movies, and sex.

"My owner came home last night, and he was in a really bad mood. Apparently there was some bad business thing or whatever, so I had to work really, really hard to get his mind back on what's really important."

"Coming on you?" asked another one of the bimbos, giggling.

That's when Sabrina realized something. None of the other women had on collars.

Kylie must've noticed the flicker of surprise on Sabrina's face. She leaned over. "These girls don't need to be trained. They already know how to behave."

"But you're wearing one too."

"That's because my Master likes me to remember my place at all times."

Sabrina licked her lips, thinking about that. At the same time, she wondered about Cale. Would he expect her to stay in a collar? Would he let her out? Would he expect her to socialize with girls like this?

Curiosity raged inside of her, but she didn't have a good answer. And for the moment, it seemed like the other girls were content to let the newcomer sit and observe without actually saying or doing anything.

"Come with me," Kylie whispered several minutes later. They still hadn't ordered, and Sabrina didn't quite understand what was going on, but she got up and followed her trainer.

They made their way back into the bathroom, an immaculate space with marble floors and huge mirrors.

"Lift up your skirt."

"What? Why?"

"Because I told you to," Kylie replied, making this sound like the most natural, normal thing in the entire world.

Realizing she didn't want a shock, Sabrina lifted up her skirt. "Oh, my. Your Master's going to have so much fun training you. You obviously need to be thoroughly broken, Sabrina. I don't understand how a girl like you can be so defiant all the time. What's wrong with you?" The lilting of Kylie's voice made it sound like she was talking to a puppy.

This time around, Sabrina didn't answer. She didn't see the point. Instead, she watched as Kylie reached into her little pink purse, and she took out a small vibrator. Rounded with a bulbous tip, it didn't have any buttons on it.

"What, what you going to do with that?"

"This is going in your panties," Kylie answered. "And I'm going to control it during lunch. You're going to be a good girl, and you going to think about your Master while you get horny."

Kylie stepped forward, and Sabrina retreated back. Before Sabrina could actually get any real distance between them, Kylie grabbed her phone, and she tapped the screen. That was all it took to deliver another electrical shock. The pain snapped through Sabrina's body, and she fell back against the wall.

"Are you going to fight me? Are you going to be a dumb bitch?" It sounds strange, hearing that kind of language come from a girl like Kylie.

Reluctantly, Sabrina shook her head.

No, she wasn't going to fight. No, she wasn't going to resist.

Kylie slid the vibrator down into Sabrina's panties. "You're already all warm and wet," Kylie said with a little giggle.

She pushed of the device up into Sabrina's slit. The invasion felt humiliating, but there was still that biological response.

Sabrina was enjoying this. She couldn't help herself.

Once she was satisfied, Kylie stepped back, and she touched the phone again. Right away, Sabrina's eyes widened, and she tried to call out as she expected a blast of pain. But this time, there was no bite from electricity. On the contrary, Sabrina felt that pull between her legs.

"The rules are very simple. You aren't allowed to touch yourself without permission. You aren't allowed to have an orgasm."

"Why, why are you doing this to me?"

"Because your Master told me that I need to give you a sense of desperation. Besides, I'm going to give you a little quiz after lunch. If you do a good job and answer all my questions, then I will let you have an orgasm. But if you can't, we'll have to have a conversation. I don't think you want that, do you? No, you don't want to talk. What do you want to do?"

Sabrina listened to the best of her ability, yet the pulses between her legs kept robbing her of her concentration. After a few more seconds, Kylie turned off the vibrator. Again, she did it simply by sliding her finger over the screen of her phone. It sent the signal, and the device became still.

"Come on, Sabrina. We still need to have lunch!"

Lunch was positively torture. As she sat there at the table with the other girls, Sabrina didn't really say anything. And yet, every few seconds or every few minutes, Kylie would be talking with the other girls, and she would find time to touch the screen on her phone.

Delicious pleasure would play along Sabrina's slit.

She ordered a simple salad, but she could hardly focus on any of the food on her plate. Instead, Sabrina kept thinking about when the other girl would turn the vibrator back on. Desperation clawed through her body.

At one point, Sabrina leaned over, and she started to whisper. She was starting to plead. "Please, do you think you could turn it back on? I promise I won't make any sounds."

"You aren't paying attention."

Locking her teeth together, Sabrina knew that Kylie was right. After all, Sabrina didn't even know what she was supposed to be paying attention to. The other girls kept talking and chatting, but it all seemed so inane. They were currently discussing where to get the best of lingerie.

"The place at the mall is fantastic!" squealed one of the bimbos. "Seriously, you can go there, and they have everything! You can make yourself look like a little maid girl, a nurse, or even a kitty. It's so sexy! My Master loves it!"

On and on, these women prattled about nothing.

The vibrator started up again, and Sabrina closed her eyes. She relaxed, only to remember that she needed to look around. She had a pretend that she was paying attention, yet she kept thinking about just one thing, the desires pounding through her skin.

"If you'll excuse me," she finally said, getting up. She made her way back toward the bathroom, and she walked, staring straight ahead, hoping that Kylie would let her go.

It didn't work out that way.

Sabrina reached out for the handle on the door into the bathroom. They were in the middle of the hallway, and Kylie grabbed her hand, pulling it away. At once, Sabrina glanced back down at the floor, suddenly ashamed. She was supposed to be back out in the dining room, listening to the prattle.

"What are you doing out here?"

Deeply chagrined, Sabrina didn't know what to say. She felt like some school kid who tried to sneak off of campus without permission. She almost expected to be told that she needed to go to the principal's office.

But no, Kylie already he had something far worse in mind for this young woman.

"I thought, I thought I could..."

"You thought you could sneak away. You thought I wouldn't notice."

Sabrina tried to think of something to say, something intelligent. Nothing came to mind. Her brain felt like a blank, especially while this girl stood there with her hands on her hips.

"Oh, don't feel so bad it's okay. You're learning to be dumb. You're starting to make stupid mistakes. Pretty soon, I bet you won't even remember how to do all that computer stuff you used to be so good at."

"I won't forget."

"Yes, you will."

"But here's the thing. You can't touch your panties. Don't you remember? I gave you an order, and your owner already approved it. That's why he programmed it into your collar."

Sabrina recalled the MRI, but she didn't think about what it really might mean, what it could really accomplish.

Hardening her lips into a frustrated line, she glanced to her left, then to her right. It was almost like Sabrina intended to escape, but even if she ran, she would still have that device locked around her neck.

"You can't get away, silly girl. You belong to your owner. You might as well accept it. Just learn to behave. Learn to be good. That's the best way to go."

"I, I don't know if I can do that."

"Then it's probably a good thing that he's not going to give you a choice," Kylie replied with another vicious smirk. "But don't worry. Since you are obviously going to fail the quiz, we can just skip to your punishment."

Sabrina closed her eyes, and she tried to tense up, expecting the sharp stab of electricity.

"No, this is going to be different. Come here."

Kylie walked over to the opening back out into the main dining room. She waved a single finger, motioning for the other bimbo to follow her.

Reluctantly, Sabrina trailed after her tutor.

"Do you see that man coming through the front door right now?"

At first, Sabrina didn't know exactly who Kylie meant. Then there was that little sharp intake of breath, a focal declaration that yes, indeed, she knew exactly who Kylie meant.

It took all of Sabrina self-control not to retreat back. "What's he doing here?"

"Oh, so you do know him."

Sabrina didn't say anything for a couple of seconds. Her heart kicked in her chest, this heavy rhythm beating away from one moment to the next. She wanted to hide it, but Kylie already took a hold of her wrist, ensuring that Sabrina couldn't just flee.

"Who is he?" Kylie asked, though she must have already known the answer.

Licking her lips, Sabrina had to answer. "His name is Josh Michelson."

"He's handsome."

"He's a bastard. He is a sexist jackass who doesn't think that women belong in business. I hate that man."

"Be that as it may, you're going to walk right over there, and you're going to tell him that he looks very handsome. You're going to do everything you can to get him to take you to his car so that you can go down on him."

"What?"

"And if you don't, your Master has already told me that he's going to lock you in a chastity belt and he's going to make sure that you don't get another orgasm for a long, long time."

"My Master would never do anything like that!"

"Wouldn't he?" Kylie replied, batting aside all of Sabrina's certainty.

In spite of herself, Sabrina realized that and remembered that she didn't know Kale particularly well. Maybe he wouldn't mind sharing her body. After all, she could be used by other people, only to be washed and rested before pleasing her true owner.

"No, please don't make me do this. Please, I'm not some slut!"

"Of course you are. You know you want to go over there. You know you want to bat your eyes like a stupid girl. You want to giggle at all of his jokes, and you want to make sure that he knows he doesn't need to compete with you because you can't really think for yourself. You aren't intelligent, you aren't creative, and you don't have anything to offer aside from the holes in your body."

Sabrina inhaled, and she tried to think about what she wanted.

Yes, every moment of this humiliated her like nothing else, but it also turned her on. So, so much! After a lunch where her tutor teased her with just of the possibility of satisfaction, Sabrina knew that she had to give in. She had to succumb.

"I'll do it," Sabrina finally declared, like there had ever been any doubt.

"Yes, you will. Go over there and make nice with him."

As she walked through the restaurant, navigating her way between the different tables, Sabrina couldn't help but recall everything she knew about Josh Michelson.

By all accounts, he was brilliant. Despite his youth, he was routinely interviewed by different business magazines. It seemed like every journalist in the city wanted to profile this young man. He was handsome, charismatic, and he knew how to bring in the investors.

Sabrina generally didn't care about the other CEOs in the city. The most part, she dealt with her own people, and she didn't worry about what the other companies were doing. So long as her own venture succeeded, she didn't need to compare paychecks or anything like that.

Except she had been invited to participate on a panel at a local college. She had gone, thinking that it would basically be an act of charity. She wanted to give something back.

From the first remarks, Sabrina and the Josh had argued ceaselessly. They discussed what both men and women could offer the workplace.

Even though it had been more than a year ago, Sabrina could still remember how he had been so incredibly smug. "Don't get me wrong. Women can be incredibly intelligent. They have a lot they can offer, but it has always been my experience that they lack a certain creative ambition. Women generally don't want to take risks. Now, I don't claim to understand the cause. Maybe it is the generalized sexism of our society. Or maybe women really don't have what it takes to challenge systemic norms. In any case, I generally prefer to hire men because men are more innovative. That's just how things are."

Sabrina tried to argue. And yet, when she looked out into the audience, she could tell that no one was really listening to her. Even the women in the audience seemed more enthralled by the things that Josh Michelson told them.

And now, she was walking over to him. She could feel the lipstick on her mouth, the blush along her cheeks, and the mascara around her eyes. Not only that, her hair was now blonde, matching her blue eyes perfectly. She didn't look like a respectable businesswoman.

No, she was just a silly girl, and now she had to talk to her rival.

"Hello," Sabrina said.

"Hello," he replied, sweeping his gaze up and down the length of her body. Sabrina practically shivered with rage when his eyes settled along her chest.

At first, he didn't recognize her. Then again, it was going to be difficult considering that he was studying the contours of her tight frame. Perhaps Kylie really did know what she was doing because he obviously enjoyed everything he saw.

"Do you think I can join you?" Sabrina finally asked. She hated feeling like a piece of meat.

"Well, I am a very busy man. Can you make sure that it'll be worth my while?" Josh asked.

Sabrina could hardly believe it. There she was, a hot girl, and he was going to question her? What the hell was wrong with this man?

"I'll do my best," she promised.

"Good girl," he told her, and he held out his hand. Sabrina hated this, but she didn't have any choice. She allowed him to guide her back through the restaurant, and Sabrina sat down at one of the small tables over by the windows.

"You look good," he told her. "But I'd love to know what's going on with you, Sabrina."

Her eyes widened again, her lips parted, and she felt the color drain away from her cheeks. Sabrina struggled and floundered as a hundred different thoughts flashed behind her irises.

"Yes, I know it's you. But why are you dressed like....this?" He waved his hand along her body. The gesture struck her as somehow dismissive.

Sabrina couldn't bring herself to speak.

"You look good as a blonde," he said, and even if he appeared sincere, the corners of his eyes wrinkled slightly, conveying that derisive of note of mockery.

""Thank you."

"You still haven't told me why you came over here, dressed like that no less."

"I thought we should talk."

"What should we talk about? Your cute little company? Is that what you want to discuss?"

It required all of Sabrina self-control not to jump across the table to throttle this arrogant jackass.

"I was hoping maybe we could spend some time together."

"You're tired of pretending to be a businesswoman, aren't you?"

"No. That's not it at..."

"It's okay. If you can't tell me the truth, you can just go ahead and leave right now." With that same dismissive arrogance, he waved her away with the back of his hand, as though she was little more than an insect.

"Fine. Yes. That's it." She uttered those words, and it felt like a betrayal. For years now, she had fought for respect and success. She swallowed, wondering if this was all worth it, and then she felt the metal around her neck.

"So you don't think you're a real businessperson? You don't think you have what it takes to succeed with the adults?"

"No, Sir."

Josh couldn't let that pass. He raised an eyebrow. "Sir? I like that. I like it a lot. Lean forward a little bit. I want to get a better look at you."

Sabrina glanced around the restaurant, almost like she hoped that someone might come and rescue her. But no, that wasn't about to happen. The only person who knew what was going on also happened to be Sabrina's tutor. And there was no way Kylie would offer any sort of assistance, not here, not now.

Reluctantly, she leaned forward, giving him an ample view of her breasts. He nodded to himself. "So, tell me, Sabrina. Why are you really doing this?"

"I was told to do this."

"Aren't you supposed to be the girl who succeeds despite all of the odds? Now you tell me that someone is just ordering you around?"

"Yes."

"Okay. I believe you." He leaned back in his chair.

"You do?"

"Yes." Only then, he leaned forward, resting his elbows on the table top. "But talking to me is only the beginning, isn't it? What else you have to do?"

"I have to give you a blow job, sir." Those words left her lips, and she could hardly believe them. Hot anger surged through her body, but it still couldn't compete with her arousal. This girl was horny; she needed relief. "So maybe we can just go back to your car and get this over with?"

Sabrina actually started to stand, but he snapped his fingers. "Where do you think you're going?"

Sabrina crumpled her brows. Confused, she looked back at this man. "I thought we would get out of here," she said.

"You made a mistake, Sabrina. You told me that you need this. If you need it, that gives me even more leverage, honey."

"What you talking about?"

"If you want to give me a blow job, you're going to have to earn the privilege. You're going to have to earn that little reward."

"What? How?" Befuddled, Sabrina knew that she wasn't thinking clearly.

"That is the question, isn't it," he told her, and he leaned back, crossing his arms over his chest. "First off, I think you should tell me that you've always been an incompetent manager."

"What? No! I can't!"

"You are already dressed like some silly girl. Just act the part, Sabrina. Tell me that you only got lucky. Your company, your IPO, all of it, is nothing but a little bit of coincidence. You just happened to be the right place at the right time."

Her lower lip trembled. Sabrina actually considered grabbing one of the knives and chucking it at him. But then she got a hold of herself. Like it or not, she had to be a good girl. Besides, Kylie was probably somewhere off in the restaurant, watching her, ensuring that she behaved herself.

"Fine. I'll admit it."

Sabrina tried to tell herself of this was just a lie. It was part of his game. It didn't actually mean anything. They were just words.

"Well?"

Sabrina exhaled through her nostrils, she opened her mouth, and she took a long, steadying breath. "Josh, I've only been lucky. That's the only reason why my company is about to IPO. I don't know what I'm doing. I'm just a dumb girl."

"Yes, you are." He clicked his tongue and shook his head. "It's nice to hear you finally admit the truth. But I think you can do even better than that."

"I thought we had a deal!"

"You thought we had a deal, but we aren't equals." Just like that, he made it sound so logical.

Sabrina really wanted to smack him across the face.

"What else do you want?"

"Get down on your knees and beg."

"No. I won't. I can't."

"Then you aren't going to get the treat of sucking me off." He spoke with an easy sense of inevitability. After all, he was in control here. He was in charge.

"Josh, I'm going to make you pay for that."

"You're some dumb blonde. You aren't going to make me do anything, Sabrina." His lips twitched with another annoying smirk. "But I would love to see you try."

She got up, and she turned her back on him, but only for a second. Something inside of her stopped, and then she faced her nemesis again. She took several steps closer, and she lowered herself down onto her knees.

"Please, Josh, can I go down on you?"

"No, you don't use my name. You address me appropriately," he told her.

Grimacing again, Sabrina forced herself to concentrate. She thought becoming a bimbo would be easy, but even with the threat of punishment and the possibility of actually getting an orgasm, Sabrina still couldn't quite force herself to do this. She hated this man with every fiber of her being, especially now that he got to see her in this *position*.

Degraded, humiliated, ashamed, and feeling so very dirty, Sabrina tried again. "Sir, can I please go down on you? Please, may I suck your cock?"

"Is that what you want?"

"Yes."

"Say it."

"I want to suck your cock. I really, really want to feel you in my mouth."

"You want to swallow my come? Is that it?"

Sabrina knew that this was a test. More to the point, if she failed at some point, he might decide to simply walk away. After all, this man knew how to be a bastard. If he really wanted to make her life difficult, then he had to understand that simply walking away would accomplish all of his goals.

But he wouldn't get to feel her mouth tight around his cock. He wanted to get to enjoy the fact that his biggest rival had been forced to blow him.

Sabrina held onto that possibility, knowing that they were the only things giving her a chance.

"Yes, I want to swallow your come. I want to guzzle it down like a dirty little whore."

"I'm sure you do," he said. He dropped some money on the table, and then he got up, and he walked back toward the doorway.

Sabrina immediately hopped up onto her feet, and she scurried after him. Because of her high heels, however, she couldn't quite catch up. He strode quickly and efficiently. He made his way back out into the parking lot, and then he got into the driver seat of his car.

Coming to an awkward stop, Sabrina halted just outside the door. She put her fingertips on the handle, and she wondered if she could really do this. Then again, she knew that she had to please her Master. If he wanted to know that he could give her any order and she would obey, then this all made sense.

Doing her best not to think, Sabrina plastered a silly smile on her mouth. She opened the door, and she scooted inside.

"There's the blonde," he told her.

"Yes, sir."

"You know, I'm probably not going to get excited until you tell me again how you never stood a chance competing against me."

That's when it finally made sense to her. Sabrina closed her eyes for a moment, and she knew that if she concentrated on those words, she wouldn't be able to get them out, not again. Instead, she allowed those sounds to simply pass from her mouth. She spoke, doing exactly what this man expected, but she didn't think about them. She doesn't think about anything at all. Instead, she experienced the arousal playing through her body, and she enjoyed the easy ecstasy of knowing that this would please her true Master.

"I never stood a chance against you! I'm just a girl!"

He opened up his fly, and his hand went down. He took out his cock, and he was already quite erect. The tip of his shaft was damp with pre-come.

"This is what you want, isn't it? You want to suck me off?"

"Yes, Sir."

He reached out without asking for her permission, and he wove his fingers through her blonde tresses. He pulled her head down between his legs, and Sabrina closed her eyes. Again, she focused on nothing. She thought about nothing.

Some part of her psyche clearly concentrated because she licked and she sucked. She hardened her lips around his shaft, just the way she expected he would enjoy. But Sabrina didn't allow any other thought to enter her pretty head.

She sucked, and she licked, and she moved her head down and up.

It wasn't long before this man decided it was time to enjoy himself. He gave himself over to the ecstasy of having this beautiful blonde beg for the privilege of offering up a blow job. So he came, spurting his load into her mouth.

For just a second, Sabrina tried to pull back. "Oh no. You're going to swallow, just like we agreed to."

Sabrina really didn't have any other choice. Bereft of options, she started to swallow.

Before the revulsion could shoot through her body, she surrendered herself to anything and everything her body wished to experience. She knew her place, so she stopped thinking again. She achieved that simple stillness, and when he finally released her, Sabrina sat up. She wiped the corner of her mouth, and she looked back at him.

"Thank you, sir."

Chapter 9

"What happens now?" Sabrina asked when she walked back into the restaurant. Unsurprisingly, Kyle he was standing there, waiting for her.

"Now you get your orgasm," Kylie said. "But first, you're going to come back and say goodbye to the girls."

To make this more difficult, Kylie pulled out her phone. She didn't punish Sabrina this time, not really. Instead, she turned on the vibrator. It was still wedged between Sabrina's legs and held in place by her cute little panties. Up to this point, Sabrina had done a reasonably good job of distancing herself from that need throbbing between her legs.

This extra stimulation made it impossible for her to think about anything else.

Fortunately for her, Kylie already knew what was happening. She had seen this many times before. She knew what the process of becoming a bimbo could look like, so she grabbed her student, and she tugged, pulling Sabrina along.

Sabrina followed obediently.

"Ladies, it's time for me to take Sabrina back to my shop. Her owner's going to pick her up soon."

"Does that mean she passed?"

"She did indeed. I'm sure she'll be joining us for lunch any day now," Kylie said, and the other girls giggled. "There's just one last thing Sabrina needs to do."

"What? What do I have to do?" Sabrina asked, breathless. Her heart kept pounding, heat played along her body, and she just wanted to climax. She didn't care about anything else.

Then again, that was the entire point.

"You need to say goodbye to every girl here, making sure to use the correct name."

Sabrina's lips parted.

"What? No. I can't!"

"Why can't you?"

Panic blasted through her. With their expectant eyes aimed in her direction, Sabrina's head blanked. She could tell the truth. Sabrina could have confessed that she didn't pay attention because she hadn't cared. These bimbos didn't mean anything to her.

A different answer popped into her head.

"Because I'm not smart enough to remember."

At once, the other girl started clapping. Even Kylie tapped her hands together appreciatively. And then when they were all done, Kylie told Sabrina to give a little bow.

Even though the blonde girl didn't understand what was going on, she played along. It seemed like the easiest thing to do.

"Ladies, someone here is going to get an orgasm soon."

The others nodded along, like this made perfect sense.

As Kylie escorted Sabrina back outside, she had to ask. "What was that all about?"

"I'm your tutor. Remember? It's my job to make sure that you learn how to be a good bimbo. Obviously, your Master will make sure that you learn how to obey and please him, but there's more to it than just that. I'm teaching you how to be dumb."

"I, I think I understand."

"It's okay if you don't," Kylie replied.

As they drove back to Kylie's shop, Sabrina kept wiggling in her seat, especially now. She couldn't drive, and she didn't have anything to think about. She kept wiggling and squirming in her seat, doing her best to think about anything except for the heat and dampness gathered right between her legs.

Sabrina had never understood how guys could complain about being so horny. But this, it felt like this primal itch deep within her body, and she wanted the relief of an orgasm so badly, so desperately.

It felt like she would have agreed to anything if it meant getting to touch herself.

When they made it back to the store, Sabrina saw another vehicle outside. It belonged to her Master!

"What is he doing here?" Sabrina asked.

"He wants to see what you've learned, obviously. Though I should warn you right now that today was only the beginning. You're going to have tutoring sessions with me every day for at least a week. We need to make sure you learn everything there is to know about being a bimbo." Kylie reached over and pinched Sabrina's cheek.

Sabrina, however, hardly noticed.

The second Kylie parked the car, Sabrina slid out of her seat, and she rushed up to the door. She tried to pull it open, only to realize that it was locked. It banged open half an inch, only to stop on the crossbar.

"Clearly, I have an eager girl," came his strong, masculine voice.

"Yes!" Sabrina cried out. She spun around, and she rushed over to her Master. She didn't know if this was allowed, but he never forbade her from embracing him, so she threw herself at him, wrapping her body around his. She pressed her face into his chest.

This moment would have looked particularly sweet at a train station or an airport.

"Master, would you like to fuck me? Please, please? I promise, I'll be such a good girl for you! You won't have to worry about anything. I won't try to think for myself at all! I promise! I've learned how to be a good girl."

"That's not entirely true," Kylie said, getting out of her car. The other woman approached and explained, "I do believe that your little bimbo here has learned a lot, but she can learn even more."

"So tomorrow? Same time?"

"That sounds wonderful," Kylie replied, unlocking the door to her shop.

"I have to come back?"

"Yes, you do," Cale told his bimbo.

He kept looking down at her, perhaps waiting for some sign of disobedience or resistance.

"Yes, Master. I don't think I understand, but it's okay. I'll do whatever you want!"

"She was right. You are learning."

Then he leaned down, and he kissed his little bimbo slave.

Sabrina savored his touch, the feel and strength of his body, but it wasn't enough.

She was in another car, in the back seat this time. She kept tapping her fingers against her thigh. Occasionally, she would even lift up her skirt, and she would look down. Her Master already knew about the vibrator in her panties, but he didn't allow her to take it out. He didn't let her do anything at all except sit in the back seat while he drove back to his place.

"Master, would you like me to call in sick tomorrow again?"

"Actually, that won't be necessary."

"It won't?" Sabrina asked with more than a hint of disappointment. But this time, she wasn't thinking about showing up to work with blonde hair or what the investors might think. She wasn't thinking about anyone's opinion except for her Master's.

"No, it won't be necessary at all," he told her.

Sabrina tilted her head to the side, confused, but then she remembered she didn't need to think. She didn't need to worry about any of this.

"Okay," she said, and she went back to wiggling in her seat, shifting around, but it didn't make any difference. She wasn't going to get her orgasm until her Master allowed it.

They drove back to his place, and he got out of the car. Sabrina tried to open the door herself, but she was in the back seat, and the children's lock had been engaged. She pulled on the handle, yet nothing happened.

Exasperation shot through her, but she just crossed her arms over her chest, and she pouted through the window.

"Fascinating," he said when he opened the door.

"What?"

"When we talk about extreme femininity, there are different approaches women can take. Sometimes, a woman can become a bimbo, and that means she is hyper sexualized. For the most part this is what has happened to you. Just think about how horny you are right now."

Sabrina nodded her head. Yes, she understood arousal.

"Is there something else?"

"Yes, a woman can also become much more childish. Like right now, you look more like a little girl somehow. It doesn't matter what you're wearing or what you do or what you say. There is a something very innocent about you right now." He swept his eyes up and down the length of her body.

Sabrina didn't know what she should say.

"Is that bad?"

"No, it's not bad at all. You're learning to be dumb, aren't you?"

"Yes!"

"Good," he told her. He took her hand, and he led her back into the house. She took the steps, and she felt much more confident in her high heels now.

They went inside, and the Sabrina kept bracing herself, wondering if he would just ask her to make him something to eat. But no, he took her back into the bedroom.

"Tell me, did you have a good day?" Cale pulled himself up onto the bed, he crossed his legs, and he watched her.

Obviously, he was studying his bimbo, doing his best to determine what had changed over the course of the day.

"Yes, Master. I had a very good day. I learned how to stop thinking."

"Really?"

"Yes. I did everything you wanted." Sabrina chose not to get specific. "It was really hard, but when I stopped worrying about what I wanted or thought about the situation, then it became much easier."

"I'm glad to hear it." He tilted his head to the side. "Now, I want you to take the vibrator out of your panties, but don't touch yourself. If you have an orgasm, even accidentally, there are going to be very severe repercussions."

"I'll do whatever you say," she replied, lifting up her skirt. She tugged down her panties just enough to give her access. She pulled out the vibrator, and she wasn't surprised to see that it was shining with her juices.

"Where would you like me to put it, Master?"

"Call this a test. Suck it clean."

Sabrina didn't hesitate. She put the vibrator in her mouth, and she started to lick it, to suck it, just as she had done with Josh's cock.

"Very nicely done," he said, offering her a little bit of applause.

"Thank you, Master," she said as she finished.

"Put the vibrator aside."

Sabrina complied.

"Now come over here."

She approached the bed, and he grabbed her, wrapping his arm around her waist. He yanked her up onto the bed, and he shoved her down into the mattress. The world seemed to blur and spin for a moment, but then he had his hands over her wrists. "I'm very proud of you, Sabrina. I've been watching you, and I knew that you had a lot of potential, but you are doing so well. You're learning to be such a good girl for me. You're not going to mind be my slave and my servant, are you?"

"No, Master. Never, Master!"

"Good girl. But you know, I might need to train you so that you aren't allowed to say 'No'. What do you think of that?"

"As long as it pleases you, I'll do whatever you want, Master."

"Such a good girl," he said, and that's when he lifted up her skirt. He yanked down her panties, sliding them along the length of her legs in one quick movement. He balled them up, and he shoved them down into her mouth. "I don't think you need to talk, good girl. You should probably quit while you're ahead."

Sabrina didn't grimace or argue this time. Sure, deep down, she still felt that strand of humiliation, but with her panties in her mouth, she didn't voice any of those responses.

Besides, Sabrina didn't care a second later because he started touching her. He began by gliding his fingertips along her inner thighs. He touched her lightly, gently. Every teasing sensation made her shiver. And Sabrina could feel her body respond other ways as well.

Her nipples poked out into her sweater.

He noticed almost immediately, and that's why he took his hand away from her slit.

Just as Sabrina became truly convinced that he was going to stroke her and finger her to an orgasm, he pulled his hand away, and he started to fondle her breasts. He placed his thumbs over her buttons, and he worked them, teasing her body like she was little more than a videogame controller.

Sabrina began to moan. She began to whimper and shake. She twitched under his tender ministrations, but it wasn't enough to give her an orgasm, especially when she still had that sweater between his hands and her skin.

"You look so good like this. You're almost modest, but not quite. If anyone saw you, they would be able to figure out the truth pretty quickly."

"Yes, Master." Sabrina agreed with him because he was in charge. He was the man. He was a smart one. She had to listen to him.

Before, back with Josh, Sabrina had intentionally worked to clear her thoughts and dissipate all of the intelligence from that pretty little head of hers. This time around, the arousal was enough. It burned away every shred of intellect to this girl possessed.

"I'm a bimbo, Master. Everyone should know I'm a bimbo!"

"My thoughts exactly," he said. That's why he reached back for his trousers. He dropped his fly, he pulled out his cock, and he positioned himself right between her legs. With his eyes on hers, he looked down into her beautiful face.

"You don't really want to be your own woman, do you?"

This seemed serious. For just a moment, Sabrina stepped out of her bimbo reverie. She understood that something important was happening here.

So she told him the truth. "No, I don't. I want to be yours! I want to be your slave girl!"

"You want to be my dumb little woman." This time, it wasn't a question.

Sabrina started to shake her head, and she would have spoken as well, but that's when he pushed forward, plunging his cock between her legs. Sabrina couldn't help herself. She arched her back, and she cried out as the first waves of sensation crashed into her.

At first, Sabrina didn't think she would be required to think at all. After all, she couldn't talk, not while gagged with her own panties. But he talked down to her anyway.

"This is where you belong, on your back. You belong to me, and I'm going to take good care of you. I'm going to make sure that you never want for anything. You're going to be so dumb and so happy. You're going to worry about your hair and makeup, and that's all. Every day, you'll think about how you can make me happy. And I'm going to love owning you."

Sabrina bobbed her head down and up. It was the only kind of agreement she could offer. As he pumped her, Sabrina closed her eyes, and she tilted her head back. She savored every moment. She braced herself for that ecstasy.

It came quickly.

Finally, Sabrina was allowed her orgasm, and her pussy tightened around his cock. She could feel him as he pushed forward and pulled back, every hint of friction offering her another burst of ecstasy.

She came quickly, once. But that wasn't enough for her.

As her Master worked her, Sabrina embraced the next orgasm, and the one after that. She loved every moment that she received. She was so grateful for every second.

Finally, he started to finish with her. He pumped her harder and faster, going deeper and deeper until he buried his cock. That's when he started to pulsate, his cock shaking as he used her. He finished, he pulled back, spent, and that's when he pulled his bimbo into his arms.

They both fell asleep together.

It was late when they woke up. Sabrina blinked several times, uncertain. For a few seconds, she couldn't actually remember what is real. On the one hand, she didn't know she had been turned into a bimbo slave.

But then, she started to shift, and she could feel his arms around her, holding her tight. It was like Cale had no intention of ever letting her go.

That notion reassured her tremendously.

At some point, the panties had fallen out of her mouth while she slept. Sabrina didn't try to pick them up. His eyes opened, and he saw her.

"How are you doing?"

"I'm, I think I'm good."

"I'm glad to hear it," he said. "Because I'm very hungry. You and I are going to have dinner, and then were going to have an important conversation about your future."

"What you want to talk about?"

"Not until after we eat," he announced.

"Okay. I can go cook for you then," she promised, and she started to wiggle, but her Master didn't let her go. He had no interest in releasing her, not yet anyway.

"Master!" Sabrina whined. "Please, can't I serve you?"

"Not yet," he said. Still holding her, he whispered into her ear. "Make me happy by getting naked."

When he finally let her go, Sabrina scurried to comply. She pulled off her sweater and her skirt. With the span of just three seconds or less, she was completely naked. She cuddled up to him again.

"Is there anything you would like me to do for you, Master?"

She reached down along his pants, wondering if maybe she could entice him into fucking her again. Her whole body throbbed with the prospect. She closed her eyes, and she found herself almost in daydreaming.

"No," he said, taking her wrist and pulling her hand away from his crotch.

"Okay," she huffed. "What you want me to do then?"

"Stay right here."

"Okay," she said, cuddling into his embrace all over again. It felt so good, to be imprisoned by his hold. She knew that she had a place. She knew where she belonged.

He held her like that for quite a while. In fact, Sabrina relaxed so much that she started to drift down into sleep. All the while, he held her, and he stroked her, running his fingers along her bare shoulders, over her forearms, and down to her thighs.

After a little while, however, he tapped her, and he told her that it was time for her to go get dinner started. Sabrina got up, and she obeyed.

At one point, Sabrina scurried back into the bedroom to ask her Master if she would be allowed to wear an apron.

"Only because you asked so nicely," Cale replied.

She dipped her head down. "Thank you, Master. She sounded truly grateful for this privilege. Then she turned back, and she returned to the kitchen like a good girl. Sabrina pulled on an apron, she didn't have anything else covering her body. At first, she was a little bit cold, but she compensated by moving quickly.

She found some steaks in the fridge, and she cooked to them up to the best of her ability. She also heated up some broccoli and she made some rice. All the while, she knew that her Master was elsewhere in the house, working or enjoying himself while she toiled.

When she finished, Sabrina searched through the house. She knocked on each door, and then she heard his voice. "Come in."

Sabrina barely looked around. She entered the room, she leaned forward slightly, holding her hands in front of her. "Master, your dinner is ready."

"Good," he said. "I'm very hungry." Even so, he didn't stand right away. Instead, he glanced from her pretty face back to his computer screen. Obviously, whatever he was working on would be of no interest to Sabrina herself.

"Me too."

Cale got up, he closed his laptop, and Sabrina had to wonder what he was working on.

"Come on," he said to his bimbo. "Let's go." Her Master squeezed her ass, nudging her forward. Like a good girl, Sabrina went back into the dining room with him. Cale was quite pleased to find his meal already there, waiting and steaming.

"Nicely done," he said to her. He sat down, and Sabrina kneeled at his side. She waited as he cut through the first bite. Her mouth was watering, but Sabrina didn't ask for any herself. She knew that her Master would feed her when he was ready.

"Very good," he told her. "Obviously, you were never meant to the executive. You should have been a servant all along."

"Yes, Master. Thank you, Master."

He took his first bite, and Sabrina waited. Then he smiled down at her, and she let out a little puff of relief. Her Master liked her work! She was a lucky girl.

As he ate, he would glance down at her occasionally, but Sabrina didn't say anything. She just watched him, grateful that she had an owner who would take care of her and tell her what to do.

It was easy this way, obeying.

As a businesswoman, Sabrina constantly had to think. She had to strategize and worry about how different companies and ideas would interact. Not now, not anymore.

That's when something occurred to her. "Master?"

"What is it, Sabrina?"

"You said that you didn't want me to call in sick for tomorrow?"

"That's right."

"So you want me to go to work?"

"Yes, we are both going into the office tomorrow."

"But, I can't, not like this."

"We'll talk about it after I'm done," he said. That's when he cut off another bite sized chunk of steak. He stabbed it with his fork, and he held it down for her. Sabrina leaned in, and she took a bite, grateful for the succulent meat. It felt so good...

In fact, Sabrina stopped worrying about work. As far as she was concerned, nothing had to exist outside of that dining room because her Master was here.

As her Master fed her one morsel at a time, Sabrina kept wondering what he had planned for her.

"Have you had enough to eat?"

"Yes, Master," she answered truthfully.

"Stand. Place your hands on the table and bend forward."

Tentatively, she pushed herself back up onto her feet, and she complied. She pressed her palms into the tabletop, and she relaxed as much as she could. Her heart started to beat more quickly.

"How much of this belongs to me?" Cale asked her as he moved his fingers along her body. He started at the back of her legs, and he dragged his fingertips up to the contours of her naked ass. Then he came closer, and he pressed his erection up against her body.

A shiver of desire sprinted through her skin. "All of it. All of me," she confessed.

"That's right. We still need to talk about the timeframe, don't we?"

"I, I don't understand," Sabrina said.

His hand cocked back, and then he smacked her bottom. Hard. Pain flashed through her skin, and she could feel the red blush play along her ass. "That's what you get for trying to lie to your Master. You know exactly what I'm talking about, slut."

Sabrina grimaced, but she didn't know what she was supposed to say. More importantly, she didn't know what her Master wished to hear. If she didn't know how to please him, then she didn't know what to say.

"I, I will tell you whatever you want to hear!"

"You're a good girl," he said. He grabbed her hair, and he pulled her head back. Another shot of pain flashed through her scalp, but Sabrina didn't know what to do. With his free hand, he smacked her ass again.

"You're a good girl, but there's still something you don't want to face. There's something you tried to lie about. What was it?"

Her eyes watered, but Sabrina didn't think she could actually utter those words.

He smacked her ass again and again. One, two, three more times. Every time his palm landed against her skin, she flinched. Her eyes watered, blurring her vision until she couldn't see straight. The world seemed to spin around her, but Sabrina still didn't know what to think.

"Why did you try to lie to me?"

On some level, Sabrina couldn't imagine lying to her Master. And yet, there was still that question lurking at the back of her mind, the one that terrified her even more than the prospect of this sort of punishment.

He smacked her ass several more times, his hand flashing down against her skin. The sounds of applause filled the room as he struck. Each blow sent another shiver of pain drilling through her body. She couldn't ignore those sensations. She couldn't fight them.

"Why did you try to lie to me?" Cale asked again.

He grabbed her ass, he squeezed, and then he pulled back.

Sabrina tensed up, thinking that she was going to get another spanking.

Instead, he came up to her, and he stroked her buttocks lightly. Just a second before, he used his hands to spank her. Now he caressed her. Every soft, gliding little touch made her shake. Her nipples stiffened, her pussy moistened, and Sabrina tried to think of something to do, something to say.

The truth spilled out, tumbling from her lips. "I don't know how long this is going to last!" Sabrina cried out, turning all of those words into one jumbled syllable.

He pulled his hands away, and then he yanked her back into his arms. He held her tight, squeezing her.

"Come with me," he said. In the next instant, Cale released his bimbo, and she looked around the room. She didn't think twice. She chased after her Master, doing her best to remain a respectful distance away.

He brought her back into the office, and he held the door for her. "Go sit at my desk. Turn on the computer. You're going to see a contract. Read it."

Sabrina crossed of the room, and she could feel her heart kicking in her chest with every step. She kept worrying that her body might rebel against her, that she might trip or collapse, that her fear might get the best of her, and she would stop. She could even refuse to turn around.

Reluctantly, she lowered herself down onto the seat, and she turned the laptop back on. She opened the screen, and that's when she saw the document.

Her Master stood a few feet away, but he doesn't say anything.

Sabrina read through one clause after another. Her eyes kept scanning all of this, and it felt so strange, to focus again. While under her Master's authority, she had been entirely domestic. She hadn't worried about complicated or convoluted ideas. Instead, all of her thoughts drifted back to sex, clothing, and makeup.

Slowly, she turned back to her Master when she finished.
"It's a contract."
"That it is."
"It's a contract that says you will be in charge of my company until further notice."
"That's right."
"I don't understand." She bowed her head down.

Cale walked up to her, and he reached down, touching three fingers to the underside of her chin. He nudged her gaze back upward so that she could look into his face. Even then, she kept fluttering her eyes, like she couldn't bear the thought of considering something so important.

"Does that company make you happy?"

This time, Sabrina didn't have to think about it. She simply shook her head from side to side. "No."

"No, it doesn't. And that's why you're going to retain ownership of your company, but until you decide to go back, you're going to stay here and you're going to be my bimbo. You're going to do whatever I say. You're going to cook and clean for me. You're going to be my little sex slave."

"I don't know if this is possible."

"Yes, it's very possible."

"No, I mean..."

Cale reached down, he touched a finger to her mouth, silencing her. "Sabrina, I am your owner right now. If I tell you this will work, then I guarantee you it will work. All you need to do is print up this document and sign it. After that, you'll belong to me."

"It sounds too good to be true." Sabrina barely whispered those words, and she could hardly believe that they left her mouth.

On the one hand, she couldn't shake the chorus of voices inside of her head, all of those other imagined women who would tell her this was insane. She was supposed to be strong, successful, a professional powerhouse who could impress anyone.

But she didn't want to impress anyone, no one except her Master anyway.

"You want me to tell you what to do right now?"

Sabrina looked up at her Master. "Yes," she whispered.

"Print the document."

She obeyed.

Across the room, the printer came to life.

"Crawl over there," he said, pointing.

Almost in a trance, Sabrina slid out of his seat, and she began to walk.

"Crawl," he called out to her.

Sabrina immediately dropped down onto her hands and knees. Moving along on all fours, she made her way over to the printer.

"Use your mouth."

She got up just enough to lean down and picked up the sheets of paper between her lips. She was careful not to dampen the pages. But then, she turned around, and she started to crawl again, right back to his desk. Her eyes lit on her Master, and she did her best to please him. She could feel her breasts sway as she made her way across the floor.

"Stand. Put the contract on the desk."

She obeyed once again, just like a good bimbo. And that's when she saw the pen. He already had one selected for her. He held it out. "Sign."

"But what if I never go back to my regular life?"

"Then I guess that means you just need to be my bimbo slave forever, doesn't it?" His eyes glittered with amusement.

Sabrina took the pen, and she wrote her name on that sheet of paper.

"Go to the bedroom. Get down on your hands and knees. Someone needs to be fucked. Hard."

Sabrina immediately turned around, and she rushed back through the house. She was practically skipping along until she jumped up onto the bed in his room. She spread her legs, and she braced her weight on her elbows and forearms.

Sabrina then waited, closing her eyes. She didn't know how long this was going to take. Distantly, she thought she could pick up on the sounds of a fax machine or a scanner.

That's when she understood. He was giving her time to soak into the new truth of her life. By putting her name on that sheet of paper, she had surrendered. She had surrendered her company. She wasn't going to need to going to work tomorrow because she didn't have a job. She was no longer a CEO. She became something else.

Sabrina almost felt like an entirely different person, especially because she kept waiting for the rush of guilt or regret.

Nothing came. At least, nothing bad.

From one second and the next, all she could really focus on was the throbbing need between her legs. She was getting more and more aroused. It was a familiar sensation, and that's when she heard the door open.

"There's my slut," he said, and she could hear the excitement in his voice. "I want you to know that I have already emailed copies of the contract to every principle party. From this point forward, you are no longer the CEO of Giggle Girl."

Her mouth went dry when she heard those words.

He came up behind her, and he touched her. He dragged his fingers along the edge of her collar and down her back.

"Are you ready to learn the true meaning of obedience?"

"Yes, Master." Although he only been touching her for a few seconds, her body felt ready, so incredibly ready. She needed him to stroke her, to tease her, to touch her and squeeze her. She wanted every sensation. She was such a greedy girl.

His hand maneuvered down between her legs, and he stroked her pussy. He teased her body for just a few seconds, and the pleasure kept singing through her skin, darting and dancing between every nerve in her body.

Then he rolled her over onto her back. He shoved her down, and he told her to close her eyes.

Sabrina obeyed. That's when he reached down to one of the drawers under the bed. Cale pulled something out. With her eyes shut, she couldn't see exactly what he was doing.

The arousal continued to accumulate, spinning and swirling just below her belly.

Again and again, Sabrina resisted the temptation to ask her Master what he had planned for her. Obviously, he would tell her when she needed to know. Or worse, she might ask, but she held her tongue. It required all of her self-control, but Sabrina managed to stay silent.

She felt the straps around her wrists. He pulled them tight, and all of a sudden her legs were spread, and she had her arms trapped above her head.

"Go ahead. Struggle."

Sabrina could do that. Biting down into her lower lip, she started to wiggle. She began to squirm, twisting to the left, then the right and back again. She didn't fight very hard, mostly because she already knew that she wasn't going to be able to get away.

"Come on. You can do better than that," he chided.

Because she didn't wish to ever disappoint her Master, Sabrina started to pull harder. She tensed her muscles, and she strained with every bit of strength she possessed. She pulled as hard as she could on the restraints.

Sabrina tried to punch; she tried to kick. It didn't do any good.

"Not bad," he said. "But maybe you just need a little bit more incentive." He ran his gaze over his helpless bimbo, and he admired her. He studied the flush of her cheeks, the sight of her lips. He admired her breasts and the curves of her ass. Everything about this young woman was perfect.

Sabrina didn't stop struggling. She fought as hard as she could, even though it wouldn't do any good. She was trapped; she was stuck.

This man could basically push a button and force her compliance. Knowing this, she struggled, but it still didn't do any good. She didn't stand a chance, and they both knew it.

His finger moved down between her legs. He touched her, gliding his soft touch over her opening. Her slit was already wet. Within the span of just a few seconds, Sabrina started to moan.

He touched her, he teased her, and he worked her up. Then he stopped. He pulled his hand away.

"Why, why did you stop?"

"Because you didn't fight hard enough," he replied.

Sabrina narrowed her eyes, and she yanked against her restraints again. It still wasn't enough.

He positioned himself right between her legs. He cocked his head at an angle, and he watched her. Sabrina fought some more, kicking and thrashing about, but she still couldn't escape.

"Poor bimbo, thinking that she can get away."

"No, Master. I know I can't!"

"But I told you to struggle." He said those words, and she realized her mistake. All of a sudden, she remembered that this was a lesson in obedience. She fought, pumping her adrenaline into every yank and twist.

But after nearly a minute of fighting those restraints, Sabrina ran out of strength. She fell back down against the mattress, still tied down, still helpless.

He reached down, and he pulled the apron off of her. He threw it onto the floor, and then he considered where he wanted to touch her next. First, he caressed her flanks. Then he moved his hands up, going higher along her frame. That's when he slid his hands over onto her breasts. He squeezed and he kneaded.

He played with her, and pretty soon, Sabrina couldn't help herself. She started to moan. Then he leaned down, and he licked her nipples, starting with her left and continuing to her right. He pressed his lips together on each of those buttons. He made electrical jolts of arousal shoot through her skin.

Through it all, she still wore her collar.

He flicked his tongue along her left nipple. He watched as she grimaced and ground. Sabrina couldn't help herself. She lost all self-control.

That's when she really started to fight.

The desperation granted her a fresh wave of strength. That's why Sabrina started to thrash again. She bucked against the straps holding her down.

"Should I touch you here?" Cale moved his hand up to the base of her throat. "What about here?" He palpated her breasts again. "Or down here?" Her Master pressed two fingers along her pussy. He touched her and teased her, working her up all over again.

Closer, closer, closer. So close! Sabrina was on the verge of an orgasm when he withdrew his hand again.

"You like this, bimbo? Do you like knowing that you are mine?"

"Yes, yes! Master, I love being your bimbo!"

"Are you enjoying this orgasm denial?" After another second, he added, "Be honest."

"No," she whispered, barely shaping those sounds.

"What was that?"

Sabrina scrunched her eyes closed. She couldn't stand the possibility of truly disappointing her Master. And yet, he told her to be honest. So she followed his command, just as she always did. "No, I hate it!"

Her Master leaned forward. He pressed his knuckles down into the mattress. He leaned in, and he whispered to her, "Good. I want you to remember this, Sabrina. Whenever you think about disappointing me, I want you to recall this exact punishment. If you disobey me, then I can deny you what you crave most. Face it. Deep down, you're nothing but a horny slut. That's why you want me to touch you. That's why you want me to play with you."

Sabrina didn't know what he wished for her to say next, but it didn't matter. His hand slipped back down between her legs, and he fingered her, touching her. His digits plunged into her pussy, and he worked his touch over her swollen clit.

All of a sudden, ecstasy raced back up through her body, the familiar passion burning hot and bright through her skin. Sabrina closed her eyes, she gasped, and she panted, doing everything she could to maintain some kind of control over her mind and body.

It didn't work.

She climaxed hard, and those rushing sensations dissipated every thought.

By the time her vision cleared, her Master was kissing her. Not only that, he had positioned himself above her. He pushed forward, and his cock slid right into her opening.

He worked her.

He plowed her.

He pumped his girl hard, thrusting and pulling back, quicker and quicker.

As every sharp breath exploded from her lips, Sabrina opened her eyes, and she looked back up at her Master. There, in his primal gaze, she saw her own subservience. She saw the face of the man who had taken her and trained her and conquered her.

She couldn't have been more grateful.

He worked her until she couldn't take any more. As another orgasm washed through her, he started to climax himself. He pumped her, draining away every last shred of strength. And when he finished, Sabrina just collapsed back down against the mattress, totally spent.

"Good girl," he said to her.

Chapter 10

Sabrina stood in the elevator. Next to her, her Master held her hand. The doors opened with a ding, and she stepped out into the hallway. He walked forward, pulling on her arm. Sabrina immediately found herself staring at the floor.

Just a few days ago, she would have walked through this office, her back straight, her head held up high.

Once upon a time, this had been her domain.

As she made her way through the office, Sabrina considered how everything seemed so different and yet familiar.

"Where are we going, Master?"

"You have an announcement to make."

Sabrina didn't understand, but she assumed that her Master would tell her what she needed to know when she needed to know it. Besides, she didn't wish to speak, not now. Already, she could feel a few eyes on her. Some of her employees were starting to notice her.

She spotted the double-takes. One girl from accounting glanced up, only to smirk before jerking her head back because she realized that the silly girl in a short skirt and too-tight tank top was actually the leader of this company.

Another guy started checking out her breasts. Sabrina's push-up bra definitely highlighted her natural assets. But when he happened to catch a glimpse of her face, his brows tightened with confusion.

Sabrina could almost guess his exact thoughts. *Damn, that girl is hot. She looks like someone who'd go down on you for hours on end. Wait. Is that the boss?*

Sabrina decided that it would be best if she just stared down at her Master's feet. She didn't want to know where they were going. She didn't want to know what he would expect of her.

He opened the door, and that's when she looked up.

"What are we doing in my office?"

Cale smiled back at her. "Care to try again? You signed a contract, after all."

Conflicting and competing sensations raced through her body at those words. Something felt cold along her back, but her pussy got really, really warm. Damn. He knew how to tease her. He knew how to humiliate and arouse her.

"What are we doing in your office, Master?" Again, Sabrina was incredibly careful to keep her voice down. She didn't want anyone to hear her. She didn't want anyone to figure out what was going on.

She kept hoping that he would take her over to the keyboard, he would sit her down, and he would have her type out an email to the rest of the company. She would tell her employees, her investors, and the other executives that she was taking some time off.

The transition could be smooth. It could be easy.

"First off, I need to get all of your passwords. Second, I thought it would be a good idea for me to break in your office."

"How?"

"By doing a little bit of work here, of course." The twinkle in his eyes made it incredibly clear that he had something else in mind as well, but Sabrina didn't quite understand.

He walked over to her office, he opened it, and he strolled inside. As he turned on the lights, he motioned for Sabrina to follow him.

Fortunately, it was still early in the morning. Kyle hadn't yet arrived to work.

"Come on, slut," he called out to her.

Blush ran over her cheeks, curling at the tips of her ears, but Sabrina nonetheless stared down at the floor as she scurried forward on her high heels. She had become more adept at moving around in them.

He closed the door behind her, and he strolled over to her desk. He sat down, and he turned on her laptop. A few seconds later, he glanced back at his blonde bimbo. "What is your password?"

"Giggles82. Capitalized G, Master."

He typed in the code, and then he leaned back, apparently satisfied.

"That reminds me, from this point forward, you aren't going to be allowed to drive or use any money on your own."

"But how will I get around?"

"Don't worry. If I decide to send you out on an errand, I can give you money for a cab. If you want to go with your friends, you're going to have to earn the privilege."

Sabrina's pussy was throbbing again. She couldn't help herself. Maybe she didn't understand exactly why her body responded this way, yet it didn't matter.

He beckoned her forward, and she approached the desk. His desk. "Would you like me to write the announcement?" Sabrina asked.

"No. You aren't going to be doing any reading or writing for quite some time, I assure you. Because really, what do you want right now? If you could have anything at all, what would make you the happiest?"

"I... don't know."

"Naughty little liar," he said. "So for that, you get to choose between the collar and a spanking."

"But I don't know!"

"Both it will be then," he told her. "He pulled out his phone, and he already had the program initialized. He tapped the screen one, two, three times.

The electricity buzzed through her body, shooting hot pain through her skin. She flinched, her eyes moistened, and she fell forward. Sabrina was only able to remain on her feet because she grabbed onto the edge of the desk that once belonged to her.

Cale stood up, and he walked around her. He lifted up her skirt, and he grabbed her ass. "Any last words before I have some fun?"

"I'm sorry I tried to lie to you, Master."

"Don't worry. You're still going to get to tell me what you really, really want. Here's a hint, bimbo. It has something to do with your position in life."

Sabrina blushed. It didn't seem possible, but he knew. He understood exactly what little fantasy immediately slipped into her airhead. But then, Sabrina didn't get the chance to really consider what this might mean as his hand a flashed down, striking into her panties.

That thin little layer of satin couldn't possibly protect her from the force of the blow. He smacked hard, striking with the flat of his palm.

Sabrina did her best not to make any sounds.

"You should probably start thanking me. After all, you need to be a grateful girl."

"Thank you, Master," she said.

If she hoped that her immediate acquiescence would shorten her sentence, she was sorely disappointed. His hand flashed down again, striking into her ass. She was shoved forward, harder against the desk.

He struck one, two, three, four, five more times. His hand started from her right buttock to the left and back again. She kept going and going until he decided that he didn't like her panties. He yanked them down. "Feet up," he ordered.

He stripped her panties off altogether, balling them up and shoving them back into his pocket. "A slut like you probably shouldn't be wearing underwear anyway."

Sabrina shook her head in agreement. "No, Master. Whatever you say, Master."

He came up behind her, and she could feel his erection. He petted and stroked the contours of her ass. He played with her reddened buttocks, forcing Sabrina to shiver. Then he reached out, and he squeezed her breasts through her tank top.

"Lovely," he said. "I can't wait to see what your employees think of the new Sabrina."

"They aren't going to respect me anymore," she said, making those words into a confession.

"Well, that's obvious."

He continued to palpate and massage her rear.

While he had spanked her, Sabrina had done an excellent job of remaining quiet. And yet now, as he stroked and teased her bottom, Sabrina started to whimper. It felt so wonderful, to have those little tingles of pleasure stream along her nerves. But she was so sensitive! Her body felt so taut and tight.

Obviously, she didn't ask her Master to stop what he was doing. If he enjoyed it, that it was his prerogative.

"That's right. Make all the sounds you want," he said to her.

Sabrina obeyed. She started to moan, especially when he reached around with one hand. She no longer had on her panties, so she had no protection from his roaming fingers. First, he caressed her thighs. He stroked her pubis, and that's when his fingertips dipped back down toward her opening.

She was already wet. She probably already carried the scent of arousal.

And yet, he played with her some more. He toyed with her and fingered her, gently. At first, he barely even touched her, but it was enough to make her moan. "May I, may I come?" Sabrina asked.

She expected him to say no. "Yes," he breathed back at her.

Sabrina cried out. She didn't expect that answer, and she wouldn't second-guess her owner. She filled her lungs, and she let out a keening rush of sound.

She was a grateful girl. She was a dumb bimbo, and she didn't think about anything else. She didn't consider who might hear.

Just a second or two later, someone started knocking at the door. "Sabrina, are you okay? Is everything all right?"

Kyle!

He must have arrived at work in the last few minutes.

Sabrina didn't know what to say.

"Invite him in," Cale ordered.

"I can't!"

He smacked her ass again, a firm spanking to remind this girl that she no longer had the responsibility of making her own decisions. She did as she was told. Nothing more. Nothing less.

"Come in," Sabrina called out. With every second, she kept hoping that Cale might let her back up. At the last possible instant, he stepped away.

The door opened, and Kyle came inside of her office, but Sabrina didn't spin around fast enough. Her former assistant probably saw her ass or even her pussy...Burning bright with embarrassment, Sabrina cleared her throat. She did her best to appear dignified.

Sabrina took her time. She smoothed out her skirt, even though it was absurdly short. For a moment, she couldn't resist the temptation, and she looked down at her bare legs. She was sure other people would have called this skirt a belt. It was that tiny.

She filled her lungs, and she looked back at her assistant. "Everything is fine."

"That's true," Cale allowed. Currently, he was leaning against the edge of his new desk. "But Sabrina, don't you have something you'd like to say to Kyle here?"

"No, I don't think so," she said uncertainly.

Cale slid forward, he put his hand on the back of her neck, and he pushed her back down across his new desk. He lifted up her skirt, and Sabrina tried to pull away, but her Master wouldn't allow it. "Bad girl," he said, and he struck twice, his hand flying down against her cute little ass.

Kyle saw the whole thing. He stumbled and stuttered, like he was trying to figure out what was happening, but then Cale released his girl, and Sabrina stood up again. She held her hands in front of her, and she kept her eyes aimed down at the floor.

"What's going on here?" Kyle asked.

Cale came up behind his bimbo, and he wrapped his arms around her body. "Yes, Sabrina. Explain to the nice young man what's going on here."

Sabrina realized she didn't have any choice. She had already been spanked in front of one employee. If she continued to misbehave, it might get worse. "Kyle, I'm no longer going to be your boss. You're going to work for Cale from now on. He is the new CEO this company, effective immediately."

"What?"

"Sabrina here has decided that she doesn't want to be in charge. Isn't that right?"

"Yes."

"What you really want, Sabrina?"

"I want to belong to my Master," she said. The words left her lips, and she looked up.

Kyle looked shocked, like he didn't understand what was going on.

To help things along, Cale explained the situation. "Sabrina here has been suffering from a lot of stress. She's tired of being in charge, so I'm going to take over for her. Officially, she still owns her stock and everything, but she won't be allowed to make any real decisions. That's my job now. Isn't that right, bimbo?"

"Yes, Master. That's right."

Kyle kept glancing from Sabrina to Cale and back again. Clearly, he didn't understand how any of this would work or what it really meant. "Kyle, I want you to know that I will be a fair employer. In fact, I think Sabrina here should demonstrate her gratitude to you as well."

"What?"

"You know, I've seen how you look at her. Have you ever wondered what it would feel like for Sabrina to touch you? Have you ever wondered how would feel if she gave you a blow job or maybe a hand job?"

Kyle turned a shade of bright red. Sabrina had never seen that before. He had always been so cool, calm, and centered. But now, his lips moved, but no words came out. It was like he had forgotten how to speak for himself.

"That's right, Sabrina. Your employee here has always had a crush on you. That's why he's always worked so hard and done such a good job. He's always hoped for a little bit more."

Kyle didn't say anything. He kept looking back at her, almost like he wanted to be brave, but he couldn't quite find the strength.

"She can do it for you here in her office. I'm sure she'll get lots of chances."

Sabrina wanted to turn around and see her Master. Instead, she concentrated on her assistant. And that's when she realized something. He was struggling. He probably wanted to say something about how this was wrong or unethical. At least, that's what she assumed.

"A hand job," Kyle said.

For one, two, three full seconds, no one spoke. That's when Cale reached down and squeezed her ass. "You heard the man. Go over there and give him a nice hand job. Kyle, would you like to have a seat?" Cale motioned over to one of the chairs.

Standing there, Sabrina didn't believe she heard him correctly. There was no way that a sweet guy like Kyle would actually want a hand job.

And yet, he kept looking back at her, almost like she was an entirely different person. He licked his lips, and he turned back to her new owner. "You think we can have some privacy?"

"Absolutely." He smirked back at his bimbo slave. "Be sure to be a good girl. I'm just going to head back down to my office to clear out my things."

Sabrina watched her Master go. He opened the door, and he was stepping through. But then hope fluttered through her chest because he paused. Maybe he was going to change his mind. Maybe she wouldn't have to do this. "Oh, Kyle, feel free to spank her if she misbehaves."

He closed the door behind him.

Slowly, Sabrina turned back to Kyle. She kept waiting for him to say something. He would go on and on about how this wasn't right, how she was a beautiful, intelligent woman, and she didn't need to change a thing about herself. He would tell her that she needed to get some help.

Or something.

Instead, he stood up just a little bit, he pulled down his pants, and even dropped his boxers.

"Well?" Kyle asked.

Sabrina's eyes widened, but just for a moment. Then she realized something.

Kyle wanted her. Badly. But he didn't want a beautiful woman who would be his equal. No, he wanted a sex slave. And even if he couldn't own her outright, as Cale did, he could enjoy himself for a few minutes.

"Yes, sir."

"Sir. I like that," he told her.

Sabrina started to walk over to him, but a different idea occurred to him. "Can I order you to crawl?"

"Yes, you can."

"Then crawl over here. Obediently, she got down onto her hands and knees, and she crawled along the floor in her former office. When she came over to him, she saw that he was already hard.

Second by second, she was grateful that he didn't actually ask for a blow job. Maybe even Kyle had limits. Or maybe he just couldn't believe his good luck. Either way, she reached up with her fingers, and she started to stroke him. She moved lightly at first, barely grazing her touch over his skin.

Little by little, Sabrina realized this wouldn't be enough. She was going to have to do a better job if she hoped to satisfy this man.

She wrapped her fingers around his cock, and she started to move her palm up and down, up and down, up and down.

"Yes, just like that. It feels really good," he said to her. But then, he looked back down into her blue eyes. "Why are you doing this?"

"My master told me to," Sabrina answered, making it sound like the most natural, obvious thing in the whole world.

"That's not what I meant," he told her. "Why are you giving yourself over to him like this?" His breathing started to turn frantic. Sabrina concentrated on the hand job. She needed to do well. She had to please this man.

As he breathed faster and faster, Sabrina moved her hand more quickly. She darted her fingertips along the base of his shaft and all the way up to the tip. Already, she could see his excitement right there.

"This is what I want," she said simply, speaking the truth.

That's when he started to climax. He spurted his load, splashing it across the floor.

When he was done, Sabrina moved back. "I need to clean this before my Master comes back," she said.

Kyle got up, he pulled his pants back on, and he looked down at her. Sabrina had already grabbed some paper towels. He shook his head, almost like he was confused, or perhaps disappointed.

Either way, he left her alone to her work.

Her Master came back.

He didn't bother knocking. He just walked right through the door.

"Kyle looks sleepy. I'm guessing you did a good job," he said to her.

"Yes, Master. Thank you, Master." She would always be grateful for every compliment.

"But you know, I think I'm going to play with you before we make that announcement. Go wash your hands. Come back here and be ready to be used."

"Yes, Master."

"That reminds me, would you like to wear your panties again?"

Sabrina glanced back down at her skirt. Considering how short it was, she really wanted her panties back. Then again, she didn't know if her Master would actually allow her that sort of privilege.

"Yes, Master."

Stand up straight." She obeyed. He came back, and he held out her panties for her, down by her ankles. Sabrina stepped into them, and he pulled the satin back up the length of her legs. That's when she felt it, the little bullet vibrator embedded in her underwear.

He was going to tease her again...

At first, Sabrina tried to argue with him, but then she stopped herself before a single syllable left her lips. She inhaled, she rolled back her shoulders, and she decided that she wasn't going to attempt to defy her Master. No, she would be a good girl. She would do what she was told.

"Go wash your hands," he ordered.

Sabrina stepped out of her office, and she hadn't taken four full steps before the vibrator came to life, pulsating against her slit. The pleasure and anticipation began to stream through her body, though Sabrina already knew that it wouldn't be enough to get her off.

He was teasing her.

Not only that, those little sounds of vibrating machinery definitely attracted more attention. People glanced up at her, and their mouths dropped open. They didn't know what to make of this girl walking between the cubicles.

But after a few more seconds, they'd realize who Sabrina really was. So they didn't confront her. Instead, they just stared after her, confused by what they saw.

Sabrina knew all of this was happening, but she couldn't say anything about it, so she scurried back through the office as fast as she could. She went into the bathroom, and she washed her hands. Another young woman, an accountant, came into the room, but Sabrina retreated out as fast as she could.

When she made it back to her owner's new office, Sabrina knocked.

"He's still in there," Kyle said from his position. He narrowed his eyes back at her, almost like she had done something treacherous.

"Come in," her Master said.

Sabrina went into the room, and she saw that he was back at her his desk, typing out something. It had to be the announcement. With a few more keystrokes, he would let everyone in the company know that Sabrina was no longer in charge.

This was really happening.

As the vibrator continued to pulsate, Sabrina waited there, wondering when her Master would acknowledge her presence.

"How are you feeling?"

"Horny."

"Good." He didn't bother to turn off the vibrator. Instead, he clicked once more on his computer, and then he went back out into the office. He grabbed Sabrina by her wrist, and he pulled her back to Kyle's desk.

Apparently, people were already starting to gather around, but Cale jumped up on the desk. "Ladies and gentlemen," he called out, cupping his hands around his mouth. "Ladies and gentlemen, can you come here please? Sabrina and I have an announcement would like to make."

Employees shuffled out from behind their computer screens. They started to circle around the desk as they waited for the announcement.

To make matters worse, while he waited for the employees to gather around, her Master looked back down at Sabrina. Up until this point, she had remained utterly still, like she hoped that none of the other workers would notice she was there. Then he held out his hand. "Come on. Get up here," he commanded.

Sabrina took his hand, and she pulled herself up onto the desk as well. She did her best to keep her knees together. Even so, she was certain that almost every employee there could see her satin panties.

Swallowing, she waited, wondering what Cale would do with her next.

"Everyone, thank you for coming," he told the gathering crowd. It took nearly four or five minutes before Cale looked back at his bimbo. "Tell everyone," he whispered into her.

Sabrina parted her lips, and she didn't know what she was supposed to say. But then, he reached around, and he squeezed her tight little ass.

"Everyone, Cale here is going to be the new CEO of this company. We have already signed all of the paperwork. I'm sure you'll do a great job for him."

Just like that, Sabrina tried to retreat, but his hand shot out, and he grabbed her wrist again. He wasn't about to let her off that easily.

"And?"

Realizing that she couldn't get away, Sabrina bowed her head down, but that she was standing on the desk, with so many people watching her, she knew they would see her blush. They would notice the way her bottom lip trembled pathetically.

"Everyone, I'm stepping down as CEO of this company because I no longer capable of taking care of things. Cale is a very smart man. He's smarter than I am. He's smarter than I could ever be. I'm just a dumb bimbo."

"And?"

Really? She had to say everything?

Apparently so.

"I'm just a dumb bimbo, so I need this man to take care of me. I need him to tell me what to do and what to think. That's why he's going to be in charge."

"Everyone, I'm sure this is very surprising," Cale told the crowd. "But I'm sure we will all be able to accomplish great things. Don't worry. You're still going to get to see Sabrina around from time to time."

She blushed, thinking about how he might use and tease and play with her...

Epilogue

Sabrina woke up, and it was Saturday, and she had her Master all to herself. He had his arm draped around her. She waited for a little while, and then she scooted back down under the sheets. She tugged it down on his sweatpants, and she found his cock. She started licking him.

This is how he enjoyed being woken up. This was what made him the happiest, so she licked and sucked like an eager little slut.

This was her life now, and she couldn't wait to be taken and used. She was dumb, and she was grateful.

The End

Printed in Great Britain
by Amazon